P9-DNM-852

"Come meet Ricky. I told him to expect us."

Ty smiled and gestured Rachel and her daughter toward the porch.

Instead of looking excited, she looked scared. Worried. Good. It would be easier on all of them if she decided not to go through with whatever she was planning.

"What's your name?" Ricky asked the little girl.

Rachel patted her daughter's back and said, "This is Katie. It takes her a while to warm up to new people. Give her time to figure you out, and then you'll be sorry you befriended her. She's usually quite the chatterbox."

Ricky smiled as he shook his head. "I would never regret befriending a child."

Rachel's smile made Ty's heart skip a beat. Even though Ty didn't believe Rachel's motives in being here were pure, he did know that smile was genuine. And it took his breath away.

Maybe the real threat she posed wasn't to Ricky, but to Ty…

Danica Favorite loves the adventure of living a creative life. She loves to explore the depths of human nature and follow people on the journey to happily-ever-after. Though the journey is often bumpy, those bumps refine imperfect characters as they live the life God created them for. Oops, that just spoiled the ending of Danica's stories. Then again, getting there is all the fun. Find her at danicafavorite.com.

Books by Danica Favorite

Love Inspired

Double R Legacy

The Cowboy's Sacrifice

Three Sisters Ranch

Her Cowboy Inheritance
The Cowboy's Faith
His Christmas Redemption

Love Inspired Historical

Rocky Mountain Dreams
The Lawman's Redemption
Shotgun Marriage
The Nanny's Little Matchmakers
For the Sake of the Children
An Unlikely Mother
Mistletoe Mommy
Honor-Bound Lawman

Visit the Author Profile page at Harlequin.com for more titles.

The Cowboy's Sacrifice

Danica Favorite

LOVE INSPIRED
INSPIRATIONAL ROMANCE

If you purchased this book without a cover you should be aware that this book is stolen property. It was reported as "unsold and destroyed" to the publisher, and neither the author nor the publisher has received any payment for this "stripped book."

LOVE INSPIRED®
INSPIRATIONAL ROMANCE

Recycling programs for this product may not exist in your area.

ISBN-13: 978-1-335-48820-6

The Cowboy's Sacrifice

Copyright © 2020 by Danica Favorite

All rights reserved. No part of this book may be used or reproduced in any manner whatsoever without written permission except in the case of brief quotations embodied in critical articles and reviews.

This is a work of fiction. Names, characters, places and incidents are either the product of the author's imagination or are used fictitiously. Any resemblance to actual persons, living or dead, businesses, companies, events or locales is entirely coincidental.

This edition published by arrangement with Harlequin Books S.A.

For questions and comments about the quality of this book, please contact us at CustomerService@Harlequin.com.

Love Inspired
22 Adelaide St. West, 40th Floor
Toronto, Ontario M5H 4E3, Canada
www.Harlequin.com

Printed in U.S.A.

Greater love hath no man than this,
that a man lay down his life for his friends.
—*John* 15:13

For Ed, Brenda and Jelana.
Thank you for letting us be part of your journey. Your family means the world to us in so many ways. We're so excited to see what this next chapter holds for all of us.

For Tara. Your giving heart inspires me every day. Not just in the big things, but also in all the little ways you go out of your way to make every kid feel special. Thank you for always looking out for others, and especially for the ways you've loved my girls.

Chapter One

Bridge out.

The two simple words were one more wrench in Rachel Henderson's plans. She should have known better than to trust anything would be so easy for her. The DNA website had listed Ricardo Ruiz the Fourth as a potential relative match. Her only relative match. Based on what they had in common, she assumed he was her grandfather. A quick search on the internet revealed that Ricky, as he was called, was the owner of the Double R Ranch, a guest ranch in the central mountains of Colorado that promised to teach a new generation of cowboys about the cowboy way of life.

It seemed almost too easy, taking the weekend off and driving two hours from Denver to the sleepy little town of Columbine Springs to introduce herself to Ricky and explain her very important reason for tracking him down. She hadn't been able to find any hotels, but given that the Double R billed itself as a guest ranch, surely they would have rooms for rent.

She'd brought her four-year-old daughter, Katie, figuring that even if she struck out with her request to Ricky, they could at least have a nice weekend.

Except they'd gotten less than ten miles from their destination only to find the bridge was out, and GPS gave no alternate routes.

So here they were. In front of a café in Columbine Springs, hoping someone could help them find a way to get to the ranch.

Though the buildings in the town looked old and worn, the café was painted a bright cheerful blue and it looked inviting, a place that welcomed weary travelers and seasoned locals alike.

When they entered the café, Rachel glanced around. A couple of old cowboys sat by the window, poring over a newspaper. The place was dominated by a large coffee bar with a pastry counter. Behind it was a large blackboard displaying the menu items. As they approached the counter, an older woman wearing a name tag that said Della greeted them warmly.

"Welcome. What can I get for you today?"

Even though Della probably said those words to a hundred people a day, something about the woman made Rachel feel almost as if she'd found a new friend. Which was ridiculous, because Rachel didn't have friends. Didn't need them. Didn't see the point. She'd learned the hard way that relationships didn't last.

The door jangled, and Rachel turned to see what had to be an advertisement for a cowboy magazine walking through the door. She hated to use stereotypes, but this man completely fit the bill of the tall, dark and handsome cowboy.

Rachel shook her head. What was she doing, thinking about such nonsense? She was a single mom and had way too many other things going on in her life to be admiring a man.

"Hey, Della," the cowboy said. "Jake. Steve."

In this place, the locals seemed to know everyone. Rachel had always wanted to be part of something like that, but she'd always figured that such communities only existed on television.

She turned her attention back to the menu. "I'd like a vanilla latte. I'll also have your turkey sandwich kid's meal with chocolate milk, and the chicken salad sandwich for myself."

Della smiled at her warmly. "You've got it. What brings you to Columbine Springs? If you're looking for activities, we've got some maps from the Chamber of Commerce on the other side of the counter. Most people just pass through on their way to ski resorts or the other side of the state, but you're missing out on one of the gems of Colorado if you do that."

The older woman's enthusiastic sales pitch about the town gave Rachel hope. If anyone could tell her how to get to the Double R, this woman could.

"I came to visit the Double R Ranch. But I got almost there and found that the bridge was out. My GPS couldn't give me an alternate route. I was hoping someone could give me directions."

Della looked thoughtful. "The Double R? That's funny. I thought they were closed for their annual cleaning week."

"We are," the cowboy said, coming to stand beside Rachel. "Cleaning week is the only way we can get Ricky to take time off."

He looked her up and down, like she was an intruder. Which was crazy, considering the Double R was a guest ranch. Surely they would be excited about having guests.

"The website didn't say anything about being closed for cleaning," she said. "When I emailed to make reservations, the email bounced."

"So you thought you'd just show up?" the man asked, sounding grumpy. "That's a huge risk to take, considering there aren't any hotels for about forty-five miles in any direction."

It hadn't occurred to Rachel that she wouldn't be welcome. Granted, she wasn't sure how she was going to broach the real reason for her visit. But she thought that somehow, being there and talking to Ricky, she'd find a way to bring it up.

"I'm sorry. I didn't think about that. I just wanted to take my daughter away for the weekend to enjoy the outdoors. And I work for an ad agency, so I was hoping while we were there, I could talk to the owner about doing some ads."

Rachel knew she sounded like a bumbling idiot as she pulled her business card out of her purse and handed it to him. As it was, she still had no idea how to tell Ricky. After all, how did one ask a complete stranger to help her find a kidney donor?

But time was running out.

Ricky Ruiz was the only relative she could find, so she hoped he could connect her with other relatives who might be willing to donate a kidney to her.

She'd been on the transplant waiting list for so long, too far down to be considered a priority unless she found her own donor. Which was why she put her information into the DNA website, hoping to find someone related to her. Her mom had died when she was ten, she never knew her father and she'd spent the years after that bouncing between foster homes. Not a life story she wanted to tell anyone, least of all these strangers. She'd eventually have to tell Ricky, but she'd been hoping to break the ice first.

The cowboy looked at her suspiciously. "So it's really a sales call," he said.

Della had been preparing their food and drinks while she and the cowboy talked. Della slid the food across the counter toward her. "Why don't you guys go over to your table and enjoy your lunch? Ty, I'll get the special up for you in a jiffy."

Ty. The perfect cowboy name. He turned his attention to Della. "How do you know I'm getting the special? Maybe I wanted a roast beef sandwich today."

Della made a noise. "You always get the special. You might be some big-shot lawyer, but you're still a Warner, which means you still pinch a penny so hard it cries out in pain. You wouldn't pay an extra dollar to get the roast beef instead of the special if your life depended on it."

Rachel couldn't believe Della was being so forward with the man, but he laughed her off. "Yes, but those dollars saved add up, and it feels good knowing I've got something put aside for a rainy day."

Ty looked over at Rachel. "Let's sit. I'm the attorney for the Double R. I protect Ricky's interests. Give me your pitch, and if I like it, I'll make sure you get out there."

An attorney. She should have known that the cute cowboy in the café would have some fatal flaw. At least now she wouldn't be tempted to think about him in any quasi-romantic way. Katie's father had been an attorney, and it had nearly ruined Rachel's life.

The stubborn look Ty gave Rachel told her that he meant business. Knowing he was an attorney made her even more certain that convincing him to let her go to the ranch wasn't going to be an easy task.

Katie had scampered off to a corner of the café labeled the Kiddie Corral that had various games and activities for children. This must be a center of community activity. Rachel called Katie over and they all sat at a nearby table.

Once she got Katie settled with her lunch, Rachel turned her attention to Ty.

"I meant what I said about wanting to get Katie out in nature. That's the appeal of the Double R to me," Rachel said. "Regardless of whether or not you let me pitch my ideas to Ricky, I still want to visit. When I was searching online for ranches and places I could take Katie, I liked the idea of keeping the cowboy tradition alive. It seems like a waste for people to not know about it."

That, and if she couldn't convince Ty to show her how to get to the ranch, she wasn't sure how she was going to talk to Ricky and ask him about other relatives. The email had bounced, and no one had answered the phone when she'd tried to call. She had no idea how they stayed in business with such poor customer service. But from the way Ty looked at her, that probably wouldn't be a good thing for her to say right off the bat.

"We must be doing something right. You found it," Ty said.

Rachel sighed. "Only after looking through three pages of search results. If you want to get your business going, you need to have it ranking higher in the search engines. Add some advertising, follow the suggestions I have, and your business will explode."

Ty took a sip of his coffee. "We do all right."

"But you could do better," Rachel said, leaning forward. She'd gone up against tougher customers than Ty, and while this wasn't her primary objective, it would help them both. "I would love to put together a proposal for you. Present it to Ricky and see what he thinks. But as I told you, that's not the only reason I'm here. I do want to take Katie to the ranch. To be around animals and in nature."

"Like I said, we're closed for cleaning."

Della set a plate in front of him with a thud. "That's not the kind of hospitality Ricky believes in, and you know it," she said. "He'd tan your hide if he knew you were refusing a little girl the chance to experience the ranch."

Ty took his hat off and ran his hand through his dark hair. "Ricky isn't the one who's going to have to deal with a lawsuit over someone not finding the ranch up to their expectations. He'll hand it all to me and make me deal with it."

Without his hat, Ty looked younger, more vulnerable. And while she'd initially thought that his objection to her coming out to the ranch was pure mean-spiritedness, the lines in his brow spoke of exhaustion.

What would he say when he realized her real intention in coming? Would her need for a kidney also create a legal hassle for him?

Ty was an attorney. He didn't have a heart. He just wanted the facts and figures, and even when he got them, he'd twist them to suit his needs.

So where did Rachel's situation fit into that picture?

Della, though, seemed more sympathetic. "You've certainly had your hands full lately. But you know how Ricky loves those little ones."

Rachel glanced over at Katie, who'd only taken a few bites of her sandwich, declared herself full, then gone back over to the children's area.

Maybe playing on Ricky's love for children was the angle she should work, instead of trying to use her professional skills.

Ty nodded. "I know, but ever since word got out that he was looking for Cinco's kid, we've had all kinds of crazies come out to the ranch, trying to take advantage of an old man in hopes they'd inherit."

He turned his attention back to Rachel, giving her such an intense glare that she was almost afraid of making her request. She would definitely do so without Ty present. From the way he looked at her, he was clearly a very good lawyer who made his opponents cower in their loafers in the courtroom.

She had no idea what he was even talking about, and she was scared. But she had no time for fear.

"You'd better be who you say you are," Ty said. "Ricky might be an old man, but he's not stupid. And I promise, if you so much as think about taking advantage of him, I will go after you with everything I have."

A lump caught in her throat. Would she be perceived as trying to take advantage of Ricky? That wasn't her intention. Based on his age, he wouldn't be a good candidate for transplant anyway. But she had to hope that Ricky could put her in contact with other relatives who might be. Surely Ty could understand a matter of life and death.

Then again, if Ty was as heartless as all the other attorneys she'd known, he might not be so understanding. And if he went after her with everything he had…

She nearly hadn't survived when Katie's father had done the same.

"I told you," Rachel said. "I'm just looking to teach my daughter about the great outdoors, and maybe, if I get the chance to pitch to Ricky, I could also land a new advertising account. I know you say you're doing just fine, but surely it doesn't hurt to look at what I can offer."

Della squeezed Ty's shoulders like she was giving him encouragement before walking away to greet new customers who had just entered the café.

"I don't suppose it would do any harm," Ty finally conceded. "But I'll be keeping my eye on you. I'll do whatever it takes to protect Ricky's interests."

Though she liked her job and her boss, Rachel couldn't see herself ever being that protective of Dan. "It sounds like Ricky is a lot more than your employer," she said.

Ty nodded. "Ricky has done a lot for me and my family. And for this community. Most of us see him as an extension of our own families. People think that because he's old and alone, he's an easy mark. My grandparents were bilked out of their savings by a con man when I was in high school. It drove me to become a lawyer. So be warned. When it comes to protecting others, I take no prisoners."

More threats. If her life didn't literally depend on it, she might have been tempted to walk away. Because somehow, she was pretty sure that if you looked at Ty the wrong way, you'd end up in court. That seemed to be her experience with all the lawyers she'd ever known. Or maybe it was her past talking—all the years spent in the foster care system with caseworkers and lawyers galore, and always feeling like no matter what they said to the contrary, none of them were really looking out for her.

Which was why Ty's loyalty to Ricky seemed so strange. None of the people who were supposed to protect her actually did, and then, of course, there'd been the whole nightmare with Katie's father. Even though Chris was dead, sometimes Rachel still looked over her shoulder for some lawyer to come after her and make good on all of Chris's threats. Though their marriage had been brief, the damage he'd done would last a lifetime. Ty might be afraid of what Rachel might do to Ricky, but in all honesty, Rachel was more afraid of what Ty could do to her. Had it not been for Chris's death, Rachel was certain she would not have her daughter.

But that wasn't the sort of thing she was going to tell Ty. He'd use it, as well as anything else she said or did, against her. Hopefully, once she got to the ranch, she wouldn't have to deal with him again. All she needed was a few minutes alone with Ricky, the chance to plead her case, and it would be enough.

What she wanted to say to Ty, but couldn't because it would reveal too much, was that she didn't have the time or energy to hatch a plot on how to bilk an old man for everything he had. She was too busy trying to stay alive.

They finished the rest of the meal in silence, and for that, Rachel was glad. Afterward, Ty led her out to the parking lot. "My truck's that one," he said, gesturing. "I assume that's you." He pointed to her lonely sedan in the sea of pickup trucks.

She nodded.

"With the bridge out, the route to the ranch is tricky, but I'll make sure not to lose you. You won't be able to find it on your own."

She nodded. "GPS couldn't even give me an alternate route."

He grinned. It was the first genuine smile she'd seen from him, and she was surprised by how much she liked it. Once again that strange feeling of attraction came over her. Crazy. Not only did she not need a romantic complication in her life, but she was certainly not going to fall for some controlling, manipulative lawyer, either. Been there, done that, and the only good thing to have come from it was Katie.

"I'll keep up," she said, ruffling her daughter's hair. Thankfully, Katie had been too young to remember the nightmares of the custody battle with Chris. But Rachel would never forget. She just hoped that she could get a kidney in time and live long enough to watch her daughter grow up. She'd always promised herself that if she ever became a parent, her child would never face being put in foster care.

But if she died, what else was there for Katie?

The custody battle with Chris had isolated Rachel from all her friends. People she thought she trusted had turned against her and spewed lies on the witness stand. Since then, she hadn't been able to trust anyone. The people she worked with were nice enough, but Rachel couldn't bring herself to form a more meaningful relationship with them than the casual pleasantries one exchanged with coworkers.

As she followed Ty off the main road onto a dirt one, she hoped that yet again, she wasn't misplacing her trust. Not that she planned on getting involved with Ty, other than following him to the ranch and convincing him that she wasn't going to take some poor old man to the cleaners.

Maybe, as different as they seemed to be, she and Ty had a lot in common. Neither trusted easily, and it seemed like they both had their reasons.

They turned off the dirt road onto another that seemed even less maintained. It was barely a step above a four-wheel trail, and Rachel had to navigate the ruts and potholes slowly. As she looked at the scenery around her, the flat plain they were on, surrounded by mountains, the nearest houses were but specks in the distance. For all she knew, Ty could be a serial killer, leading her out to the middle of nowhere to murder them and leave their bodies behind.

No one would miss them. Her boss would be concerned when she didn't show for work on Monday, and she supposed the school would wonder where Katie was. But other than that, she wasn't sure anyone would care.

A sobering thought, especially since she was fighting so hard to stay alive. Just for Katie, but Katie was important enough to make it worth her time. Worth the effort. But it also meant that unlike a lot of other people needing kidneys, she didn't have a huge network of friends and family to draw upon for donors. She was wholly reliant on the kindness of some stranger or the unfortunate passing of someone's beloved.

Before she could reflect on that further, a large ranch house peeked through the trees, and she soon found herself within what seemed like an enormous ranch compound. The photos on the internet didn't do it justice. From the majestic main building, which had to be the lodge, to another, equally impressive home that was likely Ricky's personal residence, as well as various buildings scattered around the area, the ranch looked almost like a small town.

And even though Rachel had zero connection to this place other than a positive match from an online DNA test, she had the strange sensation that she was finally coming home.

Ty had already called Ricky on his way to the ranch, so Ricky wasn't surprised by their arrival. He didn't know what Rachel's angle was, but something about her didn't feel right. While he waited for her to get her daughter situated, he'd snapped a picture of the business card Rachel had given him and sent it to one of his investigator friends.

Ricky said Ty worried too much, but that was what

Ty was paid for. Especially with all the crazies coming out of the woodwork. When Ricky's son, Cinco, had died nearly thirty years before, Cinco's wife had been pregnant. But because Cinco and his father had been estranged, Luanne hadn't wanted anything to do with Ricky. She'd disappeared, and Ricky hadn't known whether the baby was a boy or girl. He knew nothing about his grandchild, but now that he was looking at the latter part of his life, and the regrets he had, he'd been hoping to find Cinco's child to make things right.

They'd made a few announcements, put out feelers to contacts Ricky still had in the rodeo world, but no one knew what happened to Cinco's widow or unborn child.

Since then, it seemed like every other day, someone out there claimed to be Cinco's child, breaking the old man's heart just a little bit more. People heard the Double R name and saw a giant paycheck. The joke was on them. Before Ricky had decided to search for Cinco's child, he'd put everything into a trust, preserving the ranch so that future generations could learn the ranching way of life that was slowly dying out.

Ty was proud to be part of this tradition. Having grown up in Columbine Springs, the Double R had always been a part of his life. He'd been too young when Cinco died to remember Ricky's son, but it didn't mean he didn't love the Double R.

As a boy, he and his youth group would come up for campouts in the summer and various activities in the winter, and when Ty was older, he'd spent every summer working as a hand on this very ranch.

It had been an honor when Ricky had asked him to be the ranch's attorney. Originally, he'd come to the ranch to sort out water rights and protect the watershed from encroaching developments of nearby ski areas. Ty had won that fight. And he'd won several others protecting the people and place he loved so much. While Ricky had always been a fixture in Ty's life, working together had brought them closer. Ty and his family considered Ricky an extension of their family, as did many members of the community. Ricky might not have blood relations left, but that didn't mean he wasn't loved.

While Ty fully supported Ricky's dream of finding his long-lost grandchild, he was also going to do everything in his power to keep the old man from being hurt.

As Ty pulled into his usual parking spot by the main house, Ricky stepped onto the porch.

Even though this woman hadn't made the claim of being related to Ricky, she also wasn't the first to visit the ranch under the pretext of one thing, try to ingratiate herself with Ricky and then drop the bombshell that it was all because they were truly family.

Maybe Ty was cynical. But he had good reason to be.

Something in his gut told him that Rachel wasn't telling the truth. She had an agenda, and the way she stammered over working for an ad agency told him that she wasn't being honest with him. He had that same feeling with every other charlatan who'd come to Double R. Not just with the Cinco business. Over the years, dozens of people had tried to cheat Ricky.

And Ty had sniffed out every single one of them.

Ricky had such a heart of gold that if it wasn't for people like Ty who protected him, he probably would've lost everything by now.

No, that didn't give Ricky enough credit.

Ricky was a smart man. A good businessman. An even better rancher.

But he always had a soft spot in his heart for people he thought needed him.

Rachel got out of her car, looking frazzled. With the bridge out, the back road into the ranch was tricky. In certain times of the year, it was completely impassable unless you had a four-wheel drive. But the bridge needed repairs, and the ranch was closed to visitors right now.

That was the other reason he didn't trust Rachel. What kind of fool would show up to someone's ranch, unannounced, without knowing whether or not you were welcome?

He waited for Rachel to get her daughter out of the car, and judging by the way Rachel lifted the little girl, he could tell she'd fallen asleep on the drive. How, Ty didn't know, considering it was a rough drive, but he had to admit that something about the way the little girl rested her head on her mother's shoulder made Ty's heart skip a beat.

Ricky wasn't the only one with a soft spot in his heart for children. Ty had to admit that none of the people coming here to take advantage of Ricky had tried using a child before. But it also didn't surprise him. If you'd spent much time watching Ricky in town, or even as he interacted with the guests on his ranch, you'd know how much he loved children.

If Rachel had thought to use her child as a way of earning Ricky's trust, she was a lot smarter than all the others who had come before her. He'd pay closer attention to her and dig a little deeper because she was obviously wilier than the others.

When she looked like she was settled, Ty smiled at her and gestured toward the porch. "Come meet Ricky. I told him to expect us."

Instead of looking excited, she looked scared. Worried. Her brow creased in a way that made him wonder if she was rethinking her plot to take advantage of an old man. Good. It would be easier on all of them if she decided not to go through with whatever she was planning. He sent a quick prayer to God for protection, wisdom and the right way to handle whatever Rachel was bringing upon them.

He escorted Rachel onto the porch and made introductions. As suspected, when Ricky turned his gaze on the little girl, he immediately began trying to coax a smile out of her.

"What's your name?" Ricky asked.

The little girl didn't answer. Rachel patted her daughter's back and said, "This is Katie. It takes her a while to warm up to new people. Give her time to figure you out, and then you'll be sorry you befriended her. She's usually quite the chatterbox."

Ricky smiled as he shook his head. "I would never regret befriending a child. Children are precious gifts from God. I only wish our society valued them more."

Rachel's smile made Ty's heart skip a beat. They'd had plenty of nice-looking women show up at the ranch, trying to seduce their way into both Ricky's and Ty's wallets. Even though Ty didn't believe Rachel's motives in being here were pure, he did know that her smile was genuine. And it took his breath away.

Maybe the real threat she posed wasn't to Ricky, but to Ty. It made him doubly glad that he'd already sent Rachel's info to the investigator. Women didn't just use their pretty smiles to get what they wanted from Ricky; Ty had also been burned by it. He knew better than to trust that a person's motives were really what they said they were.

Whatever Rachel was up to, her real plans would be exposed soon enough. Until then, he'd remain on guard.

Chapter Two

Rachel hadn't wanted to impose, despite what Ty seemed to think, but when Ricky offered them the chance to stay in a cute little cabin, she couldn't bring herself to say no. Especially since it was the exact one she'd been admiring on the internet. Besides, they'd been at the ranch for a couple of hours, and Ty hadn't left Ricky's side. How was she supposed to talk to Ricky about what she'd found on the DNA website and tell him about her kidney situation?

Based on the conversation at the café, it sounded like others had come to the ranch claiming to be Ricky's long-lost grandchild. She didn't know the full story, but she did have the DNA website to back up her claims. And, unlike the people Ty referenced, Rachel didn't want anything from Ricky, other than the names of other possible relatives who might be willing to help her. But how was she supposed to convince Ty that she wasn't a schemer after a paycheck?

And if she didn't convince Ty, how was she going to get Ricky alone?

She set her bag on the dresser, then turned to Katie. "Are you ready to go exploring?"

Ricky had given her a map of the property, and one of the trails was marked as being suitable for families with children. It looped around a lake and sounded pretty. It had been a long time since Rachel had had the opportunity go to hiking, and she missed spending time outdoors.

Katie grabbed the small backpack she liked to carry with her. "Maybe we'll find treasure!"

Rachel grinned. "Maybe. Let's fill our water bottles and we can go."

As she stood at the sink, a knock sounded at the door.

"I'll get it," Katie called.

Her daughter skipped to the door with the reckless joy she always had, and Rachel felt a pang in her heart. What if she didn't get to watch Katie grow up? She treasured every one of these moments, hoping they wouldn't be all she got.

When Katie opened the door, Ty stood at the entrance.

"Ricky said you were going hiking. He thought I should come with you, and you could tell me your ideas for an ad campaign."

Even though she was just thinking about how to win Ty over, she had to admit that she didn't want to spend one of the few peaceful moments she'd been looking forward to with the disapproving man. She wasn't ready to have to put up her defenses against a lawyer who seemed to be looking for a reason to tear her down. Rachel hadn't done anything wrong, but that didn't mean Ty wouldn't find something.

"I was thinking about doing the loop around the lake. It seems like it would be easy enough for Katie."

Part of her hoped he'd say it was too difficult and find some excuse to not go with them, but it only brought a smile to his face.

"The lake, huh? That's one of my favorite places on the ranch." He turned to Katie. "Have you ever gone fishing? There's a great spot just off the trail. We could catch dinner."

She'd only been fishing herself once. With one of her many foster families who'd meant well, but had never connected with Rachel. She'd spent the entire time being chased by her foster brother, who'd thrown fish guts at her. Not exactly something she wanted to relive.

But the grin on her daughter's face made it impossible to refuse.

"I've always wanted to catch a fish," Katie said.

This was why she was here. Yes, she wanted to talk to Ricky and see if he could help her find a kidney. But more than that, she wanted to make lasting memories with her daughter. No matter what happened, Katie would have good memories of her mother and know that she was deeply loved.

Rachel hadn't had those memories of her mother before she'd died, and if history was going to repeat itself and leave another little girl orphaned too soon, at least Rachel could change that one piece.

Ty smiled, and once again Rachel found herself wanting to let her guard down. He seemed almost harmless, and if she didn't know better, she'd let herself trust him.

Especially when he turned that smile on her. "I don't

want to impose on your weekend, but I do know this place like the back of my hand. If you're serious about earning our advertising business, this is your shot."

"Please, Mommy?"

Even if Katie hadn't given her such a puppy dog look, Rachel wouldn't have been able to refuse.

At least Ty was making his intentions known up front. He wasn't trying to be their friend. He was taking them on a fun outing to hear her sales pitch. Similar to when she'd go golfing with clients. Only here, it was fishing, and he'd been kind enough to include her daughter, remembering that she was also here to spend time with Katie.

"That sounds wonderful," Rachel said. "I don't have much experience with fishing, so it will be fun for us both to learn. I'm not sure I've ever had freshly caught fish."

"Then you're in for a real treat," Ty said, another smile lighting up his face. "Wanda, Ricky's housekeeper, is a whiz when it comes to fresh fish. I can cook 'em up myself, but hers are better. I'm supposed to also invite you both for dinner tonight, and Wanda told me not to bother coming unless I brought her a fresh catch."

Dinner had to be her chance to talk to Ricky. Surely she could make it through an afternoon of hiking and fishing with Ty.

"That sounds like a lot of pressure," Rachel said. "What if we don't catch anything?"

If only his eyes didn't crinkle when he grinned. "We will. Ricky just had the lake stocked, and there's not a fish out there who can resist my technique."

She imagined it wasn't just the fish who found him irresistible. But she wasn't on the market for anything, and if flirting with her was Ty's way of trying to break her, he could try, but he wouldn't succeed. After everything Rachel had been through, she was impervious to flirting.

They gathered their things, and Ty led them down a well-marked trail. It didn't take long to be mostly out of sight of the buildings. Rachel paused to take a breath of the fresh air.

"You don't get much of that in the city, do you?" Ty asked, stopping and smiling at her.

He almost seemed like a different man from the one she'd met at the café. But that had been the story with Chris, as well. Chris had been charming enough to get her to let her guard down and marry him, and then he'd flipped a switch into being a controlling monster. He'd still been charming, when it suited his purposes. Which was why, even though most people would be tempted to trust Ty, Rachel wasn't going to fall for the easy smiles and newly relaxed posture.

She returned his smile then glanced at Katie, who'd bent to look at something on the ground.

"What do you see there?" Rachel asked.

Katie held up a rock. "It's sparkly."

"That's quartz," Ty said, squatting to Katie's level and examining the rock. "We have a lot of it around here, but I think you might have found the prettiest one. Do you like rocks?"

Wide-eyed, Katie nodded. She hadn't known the attentions of a man like this. When Chris had been alive, he'd mostly been aloof, seeing his child as a status symbol. Unless it was to his benefit to make people think he was a doting dad. Everything about Chris's interactions with Katie had been fake, whereas this tiny moment passing between Ty and Katie seemed real.

As Ty explained about the rocks in the area to Katie, he seemed genuinely interested in the little girl. Rachel had grown up with a lot of fake interest, and she'd learned fairly quickly to spot a phony. Except with Chris, until it was too late. And yet, as she studied Ty, bearing in mind that he had ulterior motives in befriending them, at least temporarily, she couldn't find fault in him.

"Why don't we put that in your backpack, so your hands are free for our walk?" Ty asked Katie, reaching for her backpack.

Before Rachel could explain that Katie didn't like people touching her backpack, Katie was helping him take it off, opening it so he could put the rock in.

Katie trusted Ty.

On one hand, it was heartwarming to see her open up to a new person, but on the other, Rachel couldn't help worrying what was going to happen when Katie lost her new friend.

"We should keep going," Rachel said. "It's a long walk and we still have a ways to go."

Ty stood. "The lake will still be there. But a walk is no fun if you can't stop to admire the pretty rocks. Isn't that right, Katie?"

Katie looked up at him like he was a hero. "Mom is always in a hurry. She tells me to put the rocks down and leave them for other people."

Turning his gaze on Rachel, Ty said, "Your mom

is a smart woman. We can only take a special rock or two, because otherwise, there won't be any left for other people who need a good rock. But we chose the perfect one, and now we can leave the rest for someone else."

He winked at Rachel, like he thought he was her ally. It was nice of him not to rub in the part about her always hurrying, but he hadn't needed to say all that about leaving rocks for her benefit.

When they continued on their walk, Rachel noticed that Katie immediately reached for Ty's hand, and he took it, like holding hands with a four-year-old was the most natural thing in the world.

"You're really good with kids," Rachel said. "Do you have any of your own?"

Ty shook his head. "I wish. But I am active with the kids in our church, and of course the children of guests here on the ranch. Ricky isn't the only person here with a soft spot for children. He won't hire anyone who isn't good with kids. He thinks it's important to instill the love of ranching in a person as early as possible."

She hadn't thought of the impact of getting the children involved in the ranch, but she remembered the website talking about Ricky's vision of making the ranching legacy live on.

"That sounds like a good aim," she said. "Is that what the rock lesson was?"

He gestured at a boulder along the side of the path. "Part of ranching is knowing the landscape around you, which includes the rocks. The best way for someone to get interested in ranching is for them to pursue their natural curiosity. If someone like Katie loves rocks, who knows? Maybe she'll end up a geologist if she follows that interest. Why not encourage it? That's what makes a successful ranch. Everyone doing what they love in harmony."

That didn't sound like the cranky man she'd met in the café. "Where does being a lawyer fit into that?"

He paused for a moment while Katie stopped to look at more rocks. "Protecting the ones I love is my passion. I'm a good lawyer, and the ranch needs someone like me to make sure it's not taken advantage of. I can't rope a cow, and that's okay. Wanda can't, either, but she sure cooks up nice meals to feed the guys who do."

Teamwork. That was what he was getting at. But where Rachel came from, that kind of rhetoric only went so far. People worked together, sure, but only as far as they could to get ahead.

So what was Ty after with all his rah-rah talk?

As the path meandered through the forest, Rachel found herself relaxing even more. Ty and Katie were chattering like old friends, and while Rachel still wasn't sure she liked the idea of her daughter warming up to him so quickly, she did like how he'd point things out to Katie and patiently explain to her what they were.

More complications she didn't need in her life.

All she'd wanted to do was show up, spend a nice weekend with her daughter, talk to Ricky and find a family member who might be willing to donate a kidney. Was that so much to ask for?

Okay, fine. It was a big ask. You didn't just go up to strangers asking for kidneys. But what else was she supposed to do?

The familiar fatigue started to hit, as if her body was reminding her that she was on borrowed time. Her doctor had told her to take it easy, and she mostly tried, which was why this hike was a pleasant change. She hadn't done much of anything lately, and it was killing her. But as they rounded a corner, she could see the lake, and it would be a shame to stop now. She'd find a nice rock to sit on, and she'd feel better in no time.

Ty seemed to notice her slowing down.

"Am I going too fast for you? I got caught up chatting with Katie about the rocks and I wasn't paying attention to you. I'm sorry."

She hated the sincere expression on his face. Because that made it harder to maintain her resolve to keep her distance. Why did he have to seem like a genuinely nice guy?

"It's okay. I'd forgotten how much higher the elevation is here." Rachel gave him a small smile and paused to take a sip of her water.

"At least you're focusing on your water intake. We get a lot of visitors who don't heed our warnings about drinking enough, and they end up with altitude sickness."

If she'd trusted Ty, this would have been the perfect opportunity to explain about her kidneys and how it was crucial for her to monitor her water intake. But that would have opened her up to more questions. And revealing her real reason for meeting Ricky.

Which she wasn't ready to do.

Once again she wondered if Ty was genuinely this nice, or if he was trying to break her.

"Even in Denver, altitude sickness is a danger," Rachel said, recapping her water bottle then turning to Katie. "You should have a drink, too."

Katie took her bottle out of her backpack and did as she was told. Rachel hadn't explained the extent of her illness to her daughter, because how was someone so young supposed to understand? But sometimes she wondered if it was a mistake. What if Rachel was gone sooner than she thought?

They continued their hike, heading toward the lake spread out before them, complete with a dock. She imagined that later in the season there would be some boats there, as well.

"It's something, isn't it?" Ty asked, looking even more relaxed than he'd been when they'd started their hike. "Best view in Colorado, as far as I'm concerned."

He held his hand out to Katie. "Let's see what kind of fishing pole we can find for you."

A small shed stood off to the side of the lake, and Ty pulled a set of keys out of his pocket as he approached. The more Rachel saw of the setup here, the more she could understand why Ty had been so taken aback at her showing up unannounced. Not only did the ranch have this lake but she'd also seen the stables and riding arenas. Based on what she'd seen on the website, they had winter sports, including sleigh rides and snowmobiling. All of this must take a great deal of effort from the staff.

"The website doesn't do this place justice. This shack's a bit worn, but it's quaint," Rachel said, turning her attention to Ty. He'd wanted to discuss the advertising plan, so she might as well bring that back into focus, as opposed to the fact that she was starting to like him.

Ty opened the shed door. "Ricky had some of the

kids from the youth group build it as a school project. A few of us have told him he should update it, but he's sentimental since the kids did it."

His quick admission of it not being perfect surprised her. He'd been so defensive in the café.

"And the bounced emails and unanswered phone calls? The ranch seems like a large operation, and you say you're doing just fine, but it seems like there are some things you can do to improve it."

It wasn't her job to tell him what needed fixing, especially since she was trying to drive more business to the ranch. But it seemed like a waste of a good ad campaign if they didn't also address some of the functional issues.

"You have a point," Ty said. "I did leave a note to check on the email issue. I'll find out what's going on with the phone, as well. Our office manager quit a week ago, and we haven't found a replacement yet. We have college students who work with us over the summer and handle a lot of that stuff, and they aren't due until next month."

He sighed, took off his hat and ran his hand through his hair. "Look, I know I was rude to you earlier in the café, and I'm sorry for that. We're overloaded right now, and with all the additional nightmares with trying to find Cinco's kid, my fuse is a little short."

She spied more of the vulnerability she'd seen on his face in the café, and wondered if maybe she'd judged him too harshly. That, and the mention of Cinco again made her wonder...if Ricky was likely her grandfather, could Cinco have been her father? Her mother had always told her that her father was a good-for-nothing cowboy who'd spun pretty tales and made a lot of promises he'd never intended to keep.

And maybe some of her mistrust of Ty was that he, too, was a cowboy. A cowboy lawyer. Two strikes, which made it impossible for her to give him the chance at a third.

"So what's the story with Cinco and his kid?" Rachel asked, trying to sound casual. He might have been worthless in her mother's eyes, but sometimes she dreamed of having a father. "You've mentioned a story there, but not fully."

Ty shrugged. "Cinco was Ricky's son. Ricardo Ruiz the fifth, Cinco for short. He was a famous bull rider, killed doing what he loved best, riding bulls. Ricky didn't like that his son endangered himself, so they fought about it and eventually became estranged. When Cinco died, his wife was pregnant, but she wanted nothing to do with Ricky because of all the bad blood. Ricky let her go, thinking he didn't deserve a family after pushing away Cinco. But now that he's older, he knows it was a mistake, and he wants to make it right."

Sighing again, Ty looked at Rachel. "We went public when the investigators couldn't turn up anything. Which means we've had a lot of crazies showing up, claiming to be Cinco's child. They're all charlatans, and it breaks Ricky's heart a little more each time to get his hopes up, only to find it's a lie again."

In a way, Rachel could understand what that felt like. So many times she'd hear from the doctors about potential matches, and they'd either not work out, or someone sicker would need the kidney. No one had ever lied to her about that, but when you were faced with the end of your life, with so many unmet dreams, to have your hopes dashed was particularly painful.

She wasn't a charlatan. The results on the DNA website didn't lie. She was related to Ricky, with a close enough match that he was likely her grandfather. So why couldn't she just spit it out and tell Ty about their relationship?

Even though she'd only come to find other relatives who might be willing to give her a kidney, maybe Rachel could also help this old man right the wrongs of his past. Maybe they could even be the family to each other that they'd both been longing for.

"That's sad to hear," she said. "Ricky seems like a nice guy."

"He's the best," Ty said. "Which is why I make it my personal mission to make sure no one hurts him."

The warning in his voice told her exactly why she wasn't going to tell Ty. He still obviously suspected her of being someone who wanted to hurt Ricky.

Ty put his hat back on and entered the shed, turning on a light as he did so. The space was neat and orderly, and it was set up for people to check out various things to do on the lake in the summer.

Katie pointed out a picture of a unicorn float. "I want to do that."

Ty turned to see what she was pointing at. "The lake is too cold to go swimming right now, but maybe in the summer you and your mom can come back."

He had no right making promises he couldn't keep to her little girl.

"Are you going to let us?" Rachel asked, knowing

she sounded testy, but she also didn't know if she'd be well enough to come back this summer.

He shrugged. "If there's room. I'm not turning away a paying guest. I recommend you bring Katie back to experience all the seasons. The snow has finally melted and it's warming up, so you're barely getting a taste of the spring season. It's a great place for a child."

She didn't need convincing. But there were so many variables right now, she couldn't plan on next week, let alone next month or later in the year.

"It seems like it," Rachel said. "That would be a great angle to capitalize on for your ad campaign. It seems like the Double R is very family oriented, and even though the website mentions wanting to carry on the ranching tradition, it's not the same level of encouragement for children that I'm getting from you today."

Ty opened a locker and pulled out some fishing poles. "It's a hard balance. Kids these days want amusement parks, and we can't provide that. There are places on the ranch you can't even get a cell signal. Even though we do have satellite TV and Wi-Fi, it's only available in certain buildings. So how do you sell them on something they don't know they'll love?"

He didn't know it yet, but she had him right where she wanted him. All along he'd been trying to disarm her, to find out her weakness so he'd have something to use against her. But here he was, giving her exactly what she needed to get him to see how useful she could be to the ranch.

Which meant he'd trust her enough to spend some time alone with Ricky.

Sneaky, but she did intend on getting this ad account.

The extra money would be helpful with her medical expenses. And if Ricky could see what a competent, capable woman she was, one who wanted nothing more than to find a family connection, he'd know she intended him no harm.

Rachel smiled at Ty. "And now you know exactly why you need someone to help with your advertising. To get the parents to understand why they need to take their kids to the ranch instead of another overpriced amusement park."

"I'm listening," Ty said.

Even though Ty still had the feeling something wasn't right with Rachel, he also couldn't help liking her. She was clearly an attentive mother who took good care of Katie, and was raising a respectful, smart little girl.

As Rachel explained about appealing to parents to give their children a connection with nature instead of being constantly tethered to technology, he got out the fishing poles.

He hadn't known what Rachel would say to his suggestion of going fishing, but he was glad she'd so readily agreed. Not only had he promised Wanda something to fry up for dinner, but spending time with a pole in his hand also gave him the tools he needed to think through things. Maybe it would help him sort out why, when Rachel seemed like a nice-enough person, he had all these danger alarms going off in his head.

Ty handed Rachel a fishing pole, then turned to Katie. "Which one do you want?"

"Yellow, please," Katie said, giving him the charming smile she'd obviously inherited from her mother.

It was a shame Rachel didn't smile more. She was lovely when she did so, but it seemed to be a rare indulgence, and her smiles were almost always replaced by a scowl.

Why was she so afraid to enjoy herself and be happy?

One more reason he wasn't sure he could trust her.

But her ideas about the ad campaign made sense. He'd told her they were doing just fine, and that was true. However, Ricky's vision for the place was much bigger, and they were only doing a fraction of what he'd hoped for. A decent ad campaign would get them the attention they needed on the ranch, and maybe it would also get people to forget about the whole Cinco business.

Yes, Ty would still look for Cinco's kid; he owed Ricky that much. But he had private investigators on it, and even though they hadn't had any success so far, surely they were close.

He led them to the dock, where he gave them a quick tutorial on how to use the fishing poles. Rachel caught on quickly, leaving him to help Katie. The little girl's questions and chattering were a good distraction from wondering more about Rachel and her agenda.

"I think I have something," Rachel said, bringing his attention back to her.

The pole was bent at an angle that told him whatever was on the other end was a decent size.

"Keep hold of yours," he told Katie. "I'll be back."

When he got to Rachel, she was struggling to reel

it in. He reached around her to hold the pole steady. "Crank the reel," he said.

It took them a few minutes, but as they reeled the fish in, the large bass squirming at the end surprised him.

"Wow," Ty said. "I haven't seen anything this big come out of the lake before. Can you hold it?"

He grabbed the net and scooped the fish up. Definitely a record for their lake. The bass flailed about on the dock.

"That's a big fish!" Katie shouted, dropping her fishing pole and running over to them.

He unhooked the fish and tossed it in the cooler. "It is."

"Can I pet it?" she asked.

"Sure." He made room for her to come in front of the cooler to touch the fish. It was good she wasn't afraid. So many people freaked out over touching a fish.

Katie reached her hand in and stroked the fish. "He's a nice fish. We should name him. What do you think his name should be?"

She looked up at Ty like she relied on his opinion.

"I don't rightly know. I've never named a fish I caught for supper before."

"Supper?" Katie looked confused. "He doesn't look like the fish we eat. That has bread on it, silly. We won't eat him. He's going to be our pet. I think we should name him Nathan. Nathan was my friend in preschool, but he moved away."

A fish named Nathan.

No, a prize-winning fish named Nathan that this little girl wanted to make a pet of. As in, not bring back to Wanda to cook for supper. Though if Ricky saw the fish, he'd probably want to keep it and have it mounted, for the size of the thing.

Ty took his tape measure out of his pocket and measured the fish. A record for sure.

"Nathan is a big fish," Katie continued. "Do you have a fish bowl big enough for him? The one we had for my goldfish is too small. He died. His name was Larry."

"Sorry, kiddo, we don't have a fish tank at the ranch that can hold Nathan. The lake is his home. At least until we cook him up for supper."

Katie looked confused. "But I already told you. He's not the kind of fish you eat. He doesn't have bread on him. Those fish aren't alive like Nathan."

Right. The little girl from the city had no idea where her food came from. No clue that at one point, the breaded fish she ate for dinner were once just as active as Nathan.

Great. Now he was referring to the fish by name.

Next to him, Rachel made a strangled noise. Like she, too, hadn't considered that fact.

"Great point," Ty said, squatting beside Katie. "I think we should take a picture with Nathan, then send him back into the lake to his home. If he stays out of the water much longer, he'll die."

Which wouldn't be such a tragedy if he was going to be supper. He couldn't imagine either Rachel or Katie being willing to eat Nathan, though.

At least a picture would prove that they'd caught such a large fish.

"But Nathan is going to be my pet," Katie said. "Why else would we go fishing?"

Ty looked over at Rachel, hoping she'd help him out.

"Ty said that Nathan is too big to fit in a tank, so we can't have him as a pet," Rachel said. "Just like we can't have a big dog in our apartment."

Katie let out a long sigh. "You won't let us have any dog in our apartment."

"It's not the right time," Rachel said.

She sounded just as depressed about not having a dog as Katie did. The little girl clearly loved animals, and while he wouldn't be able to salvage tonight's dinner, he could at least help with this one.

"Why don't we take that picture, then we can send Nathan back home and I'll take you to meet some of the other animals on the ranch."

"Can I hold Nathan for the picture?" Katie asked.

This had to be the weirdest fishing expedition he'd ever been on. But he couldn't stand the thought of breaking a little girl's heart.

"Sure," he said. "You have to hold him tight, or else he'll wiggle away."

Ty gestured at Rachel. "Why don't you get in the picture with them? It'll be a nice keepsake to remind you of your visit."

Rachel looked like she'd rather do just about anything else. But she gave the sort of fake half smile he'd grown used to from her and nodded. "Sure, why not."

He grabbed the fish and put it in Katie's arms. "Hold on tight. He's really wiggly, and his slick skin will make it easy for him to slip out of your arms."

As Katie and Rachel got into position, he pulled out his phone and snapped a picture. Then the fish flipped wildly, smacking Katie in the face, and leaped back into the water. A shot he also got.

From the startled looks on Katie and Rachel's faces, it would be a moment they'd always remember. And he had photographic evidence of the size of the fish they'd pulled out of the water.

"I can't believe Nathan did that," Katie exclaimed. "He's not a very nice fish. So rude that he wouldn't pose with us."

Ty bit back a laugh. "I don't think Nathan has ever been asked to pose for a picture. He probably doesn't know how."

The little girl nodded slowly. "I never thought about that. Do you think we could catch him again so we can teach him?"

He'd love to catch Nathan again. Not to teach him how to pose, but clearly he and Katie were not on the same page.

"Not today," Rachel answered for him. "I'm starting to get tired, and I'd like to go back to the cabin to rest before supper."

Ty smiled at Rachel, hoping she understood that he was thanking her for the save, but she quickly turned away as she always seemed to do when he was just trying to be nice.

"You're always tired," Katie muttered.

The look on Rachel's face made him feel bad for her. They'd obviously had this discussion before. So far Katie hadn't mentioned a dad, and Rachel hadn't said anything about anyone else in her life. Combined with the lack of ring on Rachel's finger, he assumed she was a single mom.

Yeah, he'd noticed. So sue him. He might not trust her, but it didn't mean he didn't notice her loveliness.

"How about we go back to the cabin, and your mom can rest?" Ty suggested. "I'll get my dog, Bella, and we can play with her on the porch."

The murderous look on Rachel's face told him it was probably the wrong suggestion.

"I don't leave my daughter with strangers," Rachel said.

She had a point. He should have asked her first. Especially since Rachel still hadn't warmed up to him. But why? He'd listened thoughtfully to her advertising ideas, and he'd done everything he could to be nice to her. One more reason he had to believe there was more to her story than she was saying.

Which had him back at square one, trying to figure out Rachel's real agenda.

"I'm sorry," Ty said. "I just thought you could relax on the porch, and I could sit there with Katie and Bella and toss a few balls around. I wasn't suggesting that you wouldn't be there to supervise. Whatever you're comfortable with. I can leave you two to your own devices once we get to the cabin if you want."

His answer seemed to mollify Rachel, who nodded. "I suppose that would be all right. I don't want to impose."

She'd said that several times while Ricky made arrangements for them to stay in the cabin. But if she didn't want to impose, why had she just shown up? The weird hot and cold Ty kept getting from her didn't make any sense. But hopefully, he'd hear something soon from the investigator he'd sent a photo of Rachel's business card to that would clear things up.

They gathered the fishing things, and as Ty put them away in the shed, Rachel came up alongside him. "I should...thank you...for what you did back there with Katie. I know you were supposed to bring back some fish to have for supper. I hope you don't get in too much trouble."

Ty shrugged as he locked everything back up. "We have plenty in the freezer. I'll send Wanda a text to let her know we're coming back empty-handed."

While many places on the ranch didn't have cell service, the fishing shed did. So he quickly pulled out his phone and sent the text before they were out of range.

Rachel gave him a grateful but relieved look. As much as he hated to say it, she did look tired. Bone-weary, like she'd been through a lot lately. She'd mentioned wanting this special time on the ranch, and here he was, trying to figure out her real reason for being here.

Maybe she didn't have an ulterior motive.

After all, Katie was a good kid, and other than Rachel's presumptuousness and stumbled excuse for coming, he couldn't fault her actions. Except there was still that niggling feeling in his gut that things weren't all they seemed to be.

He'd learned to trust that feeling. Especially with a woman as pretty as Rachel. Pretty wasn't even the right word for her; she was... Ty squeezed his eyes shut for a moment and said a prayer to rid him of any thoughts in that direction. He knew better than to be interested in a woman when he had that feeling in his gut.

The trip back to the cabin was slower than the one on

the way up. Usually it was the reverse, but Rachel kept having to stop and rest. It wasn't a particularly strenuous hike, so it gave more credence to the exhaustion she said she was feeling.

Katie had once again taken his hand and was asking him all sorts of questions. It was enough to take his mind off figuring Rachel out, but not off keeping a watchful eye on her.

She was definitely not feeling well.

But she also didn't look or act sick.

What stresses could be in her life that would bring her here?

None of his business. Ricky liked to say that everyone had their reasons for their hearts needing a connection to the mountains. For Ty, that meant never leaving. But he knew, from many of their past guests, that coming here did provide a special healing they couldn't get anywhere else.

Whatever healing Rachel needed, he prayed she found it.

Just as long as it didn't involve hurting Ricky or the ranch.

Maybe he was a fool for spending so much time thinking on these things. But he loved the Double R. Loved Ricky. Sick or not, if Rachel was a threat to everything they'd built, he'd have no problem dealing with her.

But as the little girl beside him tugged at his hand and pointed to the hummingbirds whizzing by, he wasn't sure it was going to be as easy as getting rid of every other crazy who'd come by.

Chapter Three

Rachel had been so tired when they got to the cabin that she'd wanted to lie down for a while before dinner instead of letting Ty bring his dog over. She hadn't pushed herself so hard physically in a long time, and it had definitely been too much. Katie had grumbled at having to watch a movie on Rachel's laptop, and while Rachel wasn't proud of using the electronic babysitter, she didn't know enough about Ty to trust him with her daughter. For her, it was the lesser of two evils.

"Let's get ready for dinner," Rachel said, climbing out of the bed. It had been one of the most comfortable beds she'd been in, a surprise since this was a guest cabin. She'd been expecting rougher conditions, but the more she'd observed since being here, the more it seemed Ricky spared no expense in giving everyone a good experience.

Katie jumped up from the couch. "Do you think Ty will bring his dog? He said he was coming to dinner, but he didn't say anything about his dog."

It killed Rachel to have to keep saying no to a pet.

But they hadn't been able to keep a goldfish alive, and it seemed unfair, with Rachel's medical situation, to bring an animal that needed more care into the mix. Especially because, if the worst happened, what would become of a beloved dog? No foster home would let Katie bring it, which meant Katie would have to endure two heartbreaks, not one.

Men like Ty weren't genuinely interested in a relationship with a child, or with anyone. It was all about the image and getting what they wanted. Chris used to tell her that he'd stay married to her if only she'd do more to present the image he wanted. He needed the perfect arm candy, not a woman who thought for herself. And when he didn't get what he wanted... Rachel shivered.

Katie had never seen her father hit Rachel, and it had only taken a couple of times for Rachel to realize that despite all of Chris's promises and apologies, it was never going to end. Which was when she'd left. Chris had made sure to discredit Rachel in every way he could, getting people to lie about her and ultimately proving her an unfit parent. Even though it made her feel like a horrible person, she was grateful for the skiing accident that took Chris's life before the divorce was finalized and she'd completely lost custody.

Chris had been so charming when they'd first met— even later, in between the times when things had been bad. To trust Ty, who had been so gruff with her when they first met, was too much of a risk.

She'd let Katie see the dog, but she would also stand guard. Make sure Ty did not get close enough to her daughter to hurt her.

They walked over to the main house. She imagined that at one time it had been a bustling family home, and something about the thought put a strange longing in her heart she hadn't expected. Rachel had given up on the idea of having a traditional family when she realized that the happily-ever-after she thought Chris would give her would never happen.

She paused at the front door, not sure if she was supposed to knock first or just go in. As she hesitated, Ty came bounding up the front steps.

"You're just in time," he said. "You can go on in. They're probably already gathering in the dining room."

Something about the way he said *they're* put an uneasy feeling in her stomach. It hadn't occurred to her that anyone other than Ricky, Ty and maybe the housekeeper would be at dinner. But as she followed Ty into the dining room, the people gathered reminded her that nothing was ever as simple as she hoped.

Ricky broke free from the crowd and approached them. "Welcome. I'm glad you could join us. We're running a skeleton crew, and while some of our ranch hands prefer to have their meals on their own, when we're this thinly staffed, everyone eats in the main house. Even if we're busy, anyone who needs a meal is welcome at my table."

The warmth emanating from the older man made her glad she was related to him. She'd heard so many bad stories about her father that a part of her had been afraid to come.

But so far she'd found nothing but kindness and consideration from Ricky. He made her almost wish this wasn't just about getting a kidney, but finally finding a family.

"I appreciate the hospitality," she said. "I'm sorry again for intruding. Ty was kind enough to take us out earlier today, but I don't want to be too much of an imposition on his, or anyone else's, time."

By starting out with her appreciation and her desire not to be a burden, hopefully her later attempts to rebuff Ty would not be seen as rude. But by the way he watched her, even though someone else had drawn him into conversation, Rachel knew Ty was not going to be so easily gotten rid of.

"It's no trouble at all." Ricky squatted down to Katie's level. "I hope you're enjoying yourself."

He stood again and smiled at Rachel. "I always thought it was a shame that Rosie and I didn't have more children. Perhaps it was a blessing in disguise. I didn't do so well with Cinco, so maybe the other children we had would have been just as messed up."

The regret in his voice made Rachel want to tell him the truth. That they were a match on a DNA website, and while he couldn't make up for what he'd done with his dead son, he could start over with her and Katie.

But that was ridiculous. If Rachel didn't get a kidney soon, Ricky wouldn't have her, and Katie would be off in some foster home. Plus, as determined as Ty was to believe she had nefarious purposes in coming, he probably wouldn't let Rachel have a relationship with Ricky anyway.

People asked Rachel why she didn't believe in God, and it was situations like this that made it hard for her to do so. What kind of God would make life full of such difficult choices? It wasn't even her choice. She didn't ask to have bad kidneys. She didn't ask to be a single mom. She didn't wake up one morning and decide that this was going to be her life.

So where was God in all of this?

And where did it leave a lonely man like Ricky, who deeply regretted the choices that led him to losing his family?

"I'm sure you did the best you could," Rachel said. "It's all we can do. I'm sure I make a lot of mistakes with Katie, but everything I've ever done since she's been born has been for her."

Ricky nodded. "I used to tell myself that same thing," he said. "Building this ranch, growing it to be as successful as it's been, I always said I was doing it for Cinco. For the future generations of the Ruiz family. But it cost me my boy."

He gave her a hard look, like he was warning her that her path would turn out the same. But it was different. She wasn't trying to make a bunch of money or anything like that. She just wanted to live, to be there for her daughter.

Ty came up behind Ricky and patted him on the back. "You didn't kill Cinco. Once you fall in love with the adrenaline high of a bull, nothing will stop you. Yes, you made your mistakes, but you also did a lot of good. The trust that you set up for the ranch will endure long past the family line and be a blessing for generations to come."

Ricky gave him a wry smile. "I know. There's no use beating myself up for what's in the past. But today I'm feeling my age, and seeing this little one with so much promise of the life ahead of her, it makes me wish I'd spent my years differently."

The genuine regret in the man's voice once again made Rachel think she would like to have a relationship with him. She could use someone with such wisdom in her life.

She stole a glance at Ty. The tender way he responded to Ricky made Rachel pause. He seemed genuinely compassionate toward the older man. He'd said he loved Ricky like family, and seeing it in action made her wonder if Ty's protectiveness was something she didn't need to fear. Ty just wanted to make sure Ricky would be all right. If Rachel wasn't a threat to Ricky's well-being, maybe Ty would leave her alone.

So how could Rachel get Ty to understand that she bore Ricky no ill will?

A woman entered the room carrying a large platter of grilled steaks. She set it on the sideboard, then turned to Ricky. "Dinner is ready. Why don't you say grace so we can all get started?"

Ricky nodded and took off his hat. As he bowed his head, Rachel noticed everyone else doing the same.

"Dear heavenly Father, we come together today to thank You for the many blessings You have bestowed on us. Thank You for the food, the friendship and the chance to honor You with the work of our hands. In Jesus's name, amen."

Something about the older man's simple prayer stirred something in Rachel's heart. It wasn't like she had never said grace before, and she'd certainly spent time around Christians. But as she looked around the room and saw the warmth among the people gathered, it felt different.

Ty gave her a nudge. "We don't stand on ceremony here. Just grab a plate, fill it and take a seat at the table. The beef is fresh from the ranch, and a city girl like you has probably never had the like. I might be a bit biased, but you won't find tastier meat anywhere in the world."

Katie tugged at his hand. "I thought we were having fish."

The woman who brought in the meat made a noise as she approached them. "We were going to. But someone didn't keep up his end of the bargain."

Her voice was teasing, and Ty made a face. "We had plenty in the freezer, Wanda. And there's no way I would've been able to catch enough for everyone."

"I caught a fish," Katie said. "His name is Nathan. Ty said we could keep him as a pet, but he has to live in the lake."

One of the cowhands snickered. "A pet fish named Nathan? You're not getting soft on us, are you, Warner?"

Some of the other cowboys joined in the teasing, and though Ty flinched for a moment, it was obvious they hadn't gotten to him.

"I'm not going to break a little girl's heart," Ty said. "Unlike you knuckleheads."

They filled up the plates and when they went to sit, Ricky gestured at the place to his right. "Rachel. Come sit by me. Bring that little girl of yours. I want to hear about this fish called Nathan."

Rachel couldn't have asked for a better opportunity. Sitting by Ricky at dinner, he could get to know her and realize she wasn't a threat. Ty sat on the other side of Ricky, and though she still felt uneasy at having him so close, maybe he, too, would give her a break.

As they ate and talked, Rachel was surprised by the camaraderie of everyone at the table. These were all Ricky's employees, and yet they acted like family. Maybe Ricky said he was a lonely old man, but from where Rachel sat, he was surrounded by people who loved him. In a way, she envied Ricky that.

Rachel didn't have that in her life. The biggest tragedy of her health issues was that if she did die, she would do so without ever having experienced this kind of life for herself. She'd promised herself she would give it to Katie, but so far her attempts had been miserable failures.

When they finished dinner Ricky led them back out into the great room, where the back doors had been opened onto an expansive deck.

"Some of the boys are going to be playing some music," Ricky said. "We like to have live music for our guests, but the people who usually do it can't this year, so some of the guys wanted to audition and see if I like their noise well enough to inflict it upon my guests."

Ricky grinned, then stepped outside the door. Rachel turned to see that Katie had paused at a horse statue.

"Katie, don't touch," she said, scurrying over to her daughter. After the great hospitality Ricky had provided, the last thing she wanted to do was have her daughter ruin a priceless treasure.

"But it's so pretty," Katie said. "I bet it's real soft and smooth."

Ty stepped up behind them. "Cinco carved that when he was a boy."

As Rachel looked at the display, she noticed a photograph of a young cowboy hanging on the wall above the statue. "Is that him?"

"Yes," Ty said. "It was his senior picture."

Rachel studied the photograph, trying to see if she shared any features with the man who was probably her father. Would others notice the resemblance? She had so many questions, ones she'd never thought to ask, ones she didn't think she wanted the answers to. But being here, seeing a carving her father had made with his own hands, it made all the questions she'd asked as a child come racing back.

Dark eyes, like her own, and a familiarity in the expression on his face. Yes, a lot of people had brown hair and brown eyes, but there was something of her in this man. Her father.

Her mother had said she destroyed all the pictures of her father, so this was the first she'd even seen. A tickle caught the back of her throat. Why was she getting so emotional? She'd long ago accepted not having a father. Even though it would be nice to have a connection to Ricky, finding a family she'd given up hope of ever having wasn't why she was here.

Ty pointed at another picture. "That was his wedding picture."

When Rachel glanced at it, it didn't feel right. Wedding picture? Her mother hadn't said anything about her father being married. But the woman in the picture was clearly not Rachel's mother.

"Why would Ricky keep Cinco's wedding picture?"

Ty shrugged. "Luanne might not have wanted anything to do with Ricky after Cinco died, but Ricky still loved her as his daughter. Hopefully someday, we'll find the baby she was carrying, and Ricky can have a relationship with his grandchild at last."

Wait a second.

Since Rachel wasn't Luanne's daughter, somewhere out there, Rachel had a brother or sister.

"Do you have any leads at all?" she asked.

Ty shrugged. "A lot of charlatans. Luanne didn't want us to find her. I don't know why. Ricky would've taken good care of her, and the baby. But Cinco always thought Ricky was too controlling, so maybe she was afraid that Ricky would take the baby away from her or something."

He shook his head, then held his hand out to Katie. "Why don't we go sit outside by the fire? You don't want to hear about Ricky's family tragedy."

A brother. Or sister. Rachel had always envied people with siblings. Even in her foster homes, where Rachel had foster brothers and sisters, it had always seemed unfair that the actual siblings had a deeper connection than anything she could have with them. She always felt like an intruder. Even in the families that said there was no such thing as step or foster, there was definitely a difference in how she was treated versus how they were. Rachel always wanted to be part of that exclusive club. Would this sibling see Rachel as an equal? Or would the revelation that she was an unexpected sibling cause pain and turmoil for him or her?

She shouldn't be asking these questions, reflecting

on the wounds of her childhood that had been less than ideal.

Her only focus had to be finding someone who was willing to donate a kidney to her.

Ty gestured at the open doors. "We should head outside now."

She must've been staring at Cinco's picture, because he added, "I know Ricky talks about Cinco like he's a misunderstood hero, and Ricky has deep regrets of what happened between them. But don't buy into all the hype. My parents have their own stories about him, and they're not all good. He was flawed, just like the rest of us, and in some ways even more so."

She turned to him. "Why are you warning me against Cinco?"

Ty shrugged. "I see the hero worship in your eyes when Ricky talks about him. And now, the way you're staring at his picture."

So she had been staring. She hadn't meant to, but how else was she supposed to react to finally seeing a picture of her probable father?

Ty gestured toward the door. "Let's head out."

Outside, the fire was burning in the large outdoor fireplace, and though it wasn't yet dark, various lanterns and twinkle lights were already lit. The effect was charming, and Rachel found that her prickliness toward Ty was melting away in the ambience. The band was just starting to warm up, and people were milling about, sipping on drinks and talking. The crowd seemed larger than the one in the dining room.

"Where did all these people come from?" she asked.

Ty looked around the area. "I'm sure word got out that Ricky was auditioning one of the bands."

That didn't sound like the Ty who had chastised her for being here without a reservation. "You mean people just show up?"

Ty shrugged. "They're friends and neighbors. They're welcome to stop by anytime."

"Unlike me?" She gave him a challenging look, and then felt kind of stupid for it. What was she going to gain by questioning him on this? She was supposed to make friends with him, not antagonize him further.

"There's a difference between friends, neighbors and strangers. You were hesitant to leave your daughter with me because I'm a stranger. But a friend or neighbor? You'd be willing to leave her with someone you trusted. Rightly so. I don't fault you for wanting to keep your daughter safe. Just like I work to keep Ricky safe."

She knew the point he was trying to make, and it was tempting to tell him that she never left Katie with anyone other than licensed childcare providers. But that thought, rather than bolstering her position, only made her feel sad. She didn't know anyone she'd feel comfortable leaving Katie with. No one that she would invite over or feel comfortable having them drop by.

As she looked around the gathered crowd, she once again felt the sadness that had been creeping up whenever she examined her life.

Rachel had spent years telling herself that she was just fine on her own with Katie. That she didn't need anyone. But as she saw people greeting each other warmly, she wondered if she'd only been lying to herself.

Katie tugged at her hand. "Mom, there's kids here. Do you think they'll make friends with me?"

Wherever they went, Katie had a knack for making friends with every child she met. Sometimes it made Rachel nervous, letting her daughter interact with so many strangers. There didn't seem to be any harm in it in this semiconfined space, but still, Rachel hesitated.

"Over there is Leah Jackson, and her husband, Shane," Ty said. "Their boys are Dylan and Ryan. I think Ryan is just a little older than Katie. Leah's sister, Erin, is the ranch accountant. They're good people. Talking with them is Janie Roberts. She's the pastor's daughter. Her son, Sam, is Ryan's age. I can introduce you if you like."

Rachel appreciated that Ty looked at her directly as he spoke, other than to point at the various people he spoke of. "There's not a face here that's unfamiliar to me, and I know you haven't sussed out whether or not you trust me, but I can tell you that if I had a little girl, I wouldn't hesitate trusting any of these people with her. These are people Ricky knows and loves. They're like family to us."

She was the only stranger. That was what he was saying.

The boys began tossing around the ball. Katie tugged at her hand. "Please, Mom, can I go play?"

She supposed it wasn't any different from Katie befriending strange children at the park. But this wasn't just a simple day at the park. Rachel still had to convince Ty she wasn't a threat to Ricky so she could have a moment alone with the older man to explain to him what she needed. Even if he wasn't willing to connect her to someone who could donate a kidney, maybe he could tell her what he'd found out about her brother or sister.

Those were a lot of things to ask a stranger. Even if they were related but didn't know it yet.

Rachel turned to Ty. "If you wouldn't mind introducing us, I would appreciate it. I'm sure Katie would love playing with some other children."

Though Ty's warm smile was supposed to make her feel better, it only made her feel worse. He was trying to make her feel comfortable, safe, willing to let her guard down. But she knew it was only to see if she would slip and give away something that would indicate she was a threat to Ricky.

Still, as he guided her over to the people he'd mentioned, she took a deep breath and put a smile on her face. Maybe seeing her interact normally with other people would make Ty realize it was safe for her to be around Ricky, and while she couldn't see her and Ty ever being friends, maybe he would relax enough for her to finally be alone with Ricky to explain why she was really here.

Ty tried to enjoy himself listening to the band. As far as he was concerned, these local boys were better than anything Ricky had ever brought in. But as he took another sip of his iced tea, he found his gaze wandering over to Rachel. She had shamed him earlier with her question about who was welcome here. He'd certainly put his foot in his mouth back at the café. But there was something definitely off with Rachel, and he still couldn't figure it out.

One minute she was as pleasant as could be, but then

he would say or do something wrong, and she would turn prickly again. This was more than a woman just wanting to get away or snag an account.

At least Katie looked like she was having a good time. That was one of the things Ty had always appreciated about children. They didn't seem to get caught up in the same kind of drama adults did. Katie was happily playing with the boys, and though Rachel had seemed hesitant at first, she'd slipped into one of the nearby chairs and now looked content listening to the music and watching the children play.

He turned to stare at her again.

Rachel wasn't there.

He scanned the area, and Katie was still playing with Ryan and Sam. But he didn't see Rachel. For someone who seemed to make such a big deal out of not leaving her child, it seemed odd that he couldn't find her now.

Ty went over to Leah, who was smiling to the music and patting her tiny baby bump. "Where did Rachel get off to? I can't see her leaving Katie alone for so long."

"She asked if I'd look out for her for a few minutes. I think she needed to use the restroom."

Even though it was a perfectly reasonable explanation, Ty had a feeling there was more to it than that. He looked around for Ricky. Ricky wasn't in his usual spot, and as Ty scanned the crowd, he didn't see the older man anywhere.

Some might think Ty was overthinking. But you didn't get to be a good lawyer by assuming that coincidences were mere happenstance.

"If you see her, let her know I'm looking for her. I want to make sure she's having a good time."

In case he was wrong, he wouldn't alert Leah to the fact that he thought something might be off with Rachel. He strolled through the party, looking as casual as he could but searching for either Ricky or Rachel.

Neither were anywhere to be seen.

Ty went into the house, scanning the empty great room and noticing immediately that all of the partygoers were outside, not within. He quickly walked through the main floor, noting that the doors to both restrooms were open and the rooms empty. Ty spied a light on in the back hallway that led to the ranch offices. A light that shouldn't have been on. He walked back into the area and saw that the door to Ricky's office was ajar.

Ricky had a strict policy of not conducting business during his parties, and the only reason anyone would be in Ricky's office would be to conduct business. Ricky was very particular about who got to be in his office and when.

Ty pushed the door open to find Rachel standing before Ricky, tears streaming down her face.

"What's going on in here?" Ty asked.

Ricky turned to look at Ty. "She says she thinks she's Cinco's daughter. But Luanne isn't her mother. Can you believe that? This woman comes in here, takes advantage of my hospitality and then accuses my son of cheating?"

So Ty's instinct was right. Not only was Rachel not who she said she was, but she was, in fact, just another Cinco scammer.

"She did seem particularly interested in Cinco," Ty said. He turned to Rachel. "I warned you. After everything I said, you looked me in the eye, and you told me

I had nothing to worry about. But here you are, and you're pulling the most ridiculous scam anyone ever could. Have you no shame? Preying on an old man?"

More tears streamed down Rachel's face. "This is why I didn't tell you. I'm not a scammer. I did an on-line DNA test, and Ricky came back as a relative. My only relative. My mom died when I was ten, and I don't know my father. I just wanted to meet someone from my family."

If she'd been the first woman to cry in Ricky's office, Ty might have been tempted to believe her. But he knew he still wasn't getting the full story. He wasn't even sure that what she was telling him now was the truth.

"Then why didn't you just say so when we first met?" Ty asked.

Rachel sighed. "Because you were so worried about scammers. I thought that if you got to know me first and knew that I didn't want Ricky's money, you'd have been more open to getting to know me. I'm even willing to sign documentation to that effect."

This was a new one, but Ty was sure she would find some other angle to play. They all did. And poor Ricky just sat there, looking helpless.

No. Not helpless. Like his heart was breaking.

Ty went to stand beside Ricky and gave the older man a pat on the back. "Here we value honesty and openness. You should have gotten that in your conversations with us. I told you that I cared about Ricky and would protect him. So tell me. Why should we believe anything you say?"

He had to give Rachel credit for being a good actress. She brushed the tears from her face, then pulled out her phone. After punching in a few things, she held it out to him.

"That's the DNA website," she said. "As you can see, Ricky and I are a match."

It looked real. But one guy had even produced a fake birth certificate, so at this point, Ty couldn't believe it.

"How do we know it's not a fake?" Ty asked, glancing at the information and noting that the website was a reputable one that they had registered Ricky on in the early stages of the search for Cinco's child. But they hadn't found anything, and they'd gotten worried about privacy concerns, so Ty had deactivated the account.

Could a deactivated account still produce results? Ty didn't know, but he would look into it first thing Monday morning.

"How can you fake something like this?" Rachel asked. "I put my information in, did the DNA test they sent me and this is the result they came up with."

Her voice had now come to a desperate screech. He knew that desperation. He'd heard it before.

"How much will it take for you to leave quietly?" Ty asked, walking over to the desk like he was going to get a checkbook.

He wasn't, but it was amazing how many people could come up with a number pretty quickly.

"I told you," Rachel said. "I don't want money. I'm just here to learn about my family."

Another lie. He could tell by the way her voice quivered.

"What do you want to know?" Ty asked. He'd give her enough wiggle room for him to learn more about her motivations and trip her up in another lie or two.

He stole a glance at Ricky, who looked like he was

barely keeping it together. How much more was this old man supposed to endure, searching for a grandchild who clearly didn't want to be found? True, the child had had no say in the matter, but Luanne had done a good job of covering her tracks.

Rachel shrugged. "I don't know. Anything. What other family members do I have? You're my grandfather, but do you have brothers, sisters? What about my grandmother? Did she have any siblings? It sounds like I have a brother or sister somewhere. How close are you to finding them?"

Ricky glanced over at Ty before turning his attention to Rachel. "There aren't any. I was an only child. My Rosie was an only child. Cinco was an only child. Luanne had him wrapped so tightly around her little finger that he would've never cheated on her. Never. A Ruiz might talk a good talk, flirt a little for attention, but we are one-woman men. So don't you come in here and dishonor my boy's memory."

Ty knew most of this to be true. That was why he'd worked so closely with Erin Drummond in putting together a trust for the ranch. Ricky had no one to leave it to, not even a distant cousin a hundred times removed, at least not as far as they'd been able to find.

But the part about Cinco never cheating, Ty questioned. Mostly because, as he'd investigated Cinco and the life he lived before his death and during his estrangement from Ricky, he'd talked to a lot of people. By all accounts, Cinco had turned his back on the Christian upbringing he'd had at the Double R. He drank too much, partied too hard and there had been women. Lots of women.

Was it possible that Cinco had gotten one of them pregnant?

He looked again at Rachel, trying to see if she shared any of Cinco's or Ricky's features. Brown hair. Brown eyes. Warm brown skin. But half the planet had those features.

"Do you think it's any easier for me, thinking that my mother had an affair with a married man?" Rachel asked, fresh tears filling her eyes.

Ricky shook his head sadly. "I know my boy."

No, he didn't. Ty had kept that information from the old man, not wanting him to pile more guilt upon himself for not raising him right. And now Ty deeply regretted that decision. He wouldn't break Ricky's heart in front of Rachel, but he knew that at some point, Ricky needed to hear the truth.

"But the DNA test," Rachel said. "Doesn't that mean something?" Then a weary look crossed her face as she sighed. "I suppose it doesn't matter. If you're the only person left in your line and you have no leads as to who my brother or sister might be, this is it. I'm out of options. I'll just have to hope someone from my mother's side of the family will register in the DNA database and I can get…" She hesitated, then shook her head. "It doesn't matter. I should have known that this was all too good to be true."

She took a step toward the door. "I didn't mean to cause any trouble. I just needed to find someone I'm related to."

Then she paused, like she was trying to think through her next words. She turned to stare at Ty. "You want to know my ulterior motive? Fine. It's completely

useless now. I went online to search for relatives because I need a new kidney. I'm so far down on the list
that I probably won't get one in time. I knew Ricky
was too old to give me one, but I had hoped he could
connect me with other relatives who might have compassion on a single mom who's just trying to stay alive
for her daughter."

A kidney? That was definitely one Ty hadn't heard
before. But he didn't have the same suspicious feeling
he'd had about her all along as she spoke now.

Could Rachel be telling the truth?

Rachel squared her shoulders, then looked over at
Ricky. "Your money doesn't do me any good. I'm sorry
that I'm the product of your son's infidelity, but I wasn't
the one who made him cheat. I'll take my daughter and
go back to the cabin for the night. I'd leave now, but I
don't think I'd find my way in the dark. We'll be gone
first thing tomorrow morning, and I won't bother you
again."

Ty glanced at Ricky, and he could tell that her words
had hit every sensitive spot in his heart.

Once again he wondered: What if Rachel was telling the truth?

"You need a kidney?" Ricky asked. "Why didn't
you just say so?"

Rachel shook her head slowly. "You were all so
freaked out about the money. I can't imagine how you'd
feel if I had asked you for a body part. People are more
likely to part with their money than their organs."

The bitterness in Rachel's voice shamed Ty. Crazy,
considering Rachel was the one who had been dishon-

est in all this. But it seemed wrong to turn away a sick woman, especially one with a child.

A part of him wondered if this was just one more piece of the scam—Rachel claiming she didn't want any money from Ricky, and that it was all about a kidney. But what happened if down the road, she said she needed money to get someone to give her a kidney? People bought and sold organs on the black market all the time, so maybe this was Rachel's way of making herself look sympathetic so she could get the money without looking greedy.

So much to process. So many lies to sort through.

How was he supposed to believe her?

But how could he turn away a potentially sick woman and her child?

When he glanced at Ricky, he could see that the older man was having the same internal debate.

"We help family when they're sick," Ricky said. "If there's any chance you're family, I don't think I could live with myself for turning you away."

"I'm not asking for anything," Rachel said. "I got the answers I needed. I'll look elsewhere for a donor. But if you do happen to find Cinco's other child, I would appreciate you putting us in touch."

At her words, Ricky looked like he'd been kicked in the gut. Ty felt somewhat the same, but there was still part of him that wondered if they were getting the real story.

But what if she wasn't lying? Ty closed his eyes and sent a quick prayer heavenward that God would reveal the truth as quickly as possible.

"If you're really Ricky's grandchild, we'll do what

we can to help you get a donor," Ty said, giving Ricky a reassuring look before bringing his attention back to Rachel. "You don't need to run off first thing in the morning. Finish spending the weekend with your daughter. We'll do another DNA test, which I'll have sent out first thing Monday morning. If you're really related, we'll want to get to know you, and you should get to know Ricky. You're family, and family sticks together. But if that DNA comes back as proof that you're lying, we will file charges against you."

Every charlatan had balked at the idea of taking a DNA test supervised by Ty. A few had agreed, but when they realized just how closely Ty supervised the sample process, they all gave up on their golden dreams.

If the test came back and Rachel was Ricky's granddaughter, Ty would be willing to eat some crow. He'd do everything he could to help Rachel get her kidney. Ricky would want it that way.

But based on the way she'd deceived them to get this far, he wasn't ever going to trust her. If you could lie that easily about some things, you were just as likely to lie about others. And there was no room in Ty's life for liars.

He'd do what he could for Ricky's sake, but as far as Ty was concerned, Rachel wasn't someone to get close to. Except to make sure her lies didn't hurt Ricky further.

Ricky nodded slowly. "That sounds reasonable to me. I won't turn my back on family. But I do need to know the truth. And if you're lying, Ty will make you regret your actions."

Rachel paled, but she nodded slowly. "I'll do another DNA test."

"Good," Ricky said. "But just in case, Ty will be watching out for you. You'll have the same privileges as any other guest, but outside your cabin, you will be escorted by Ty at all times. Too many people come here thinking I'm going to let my guard down, and they hit me where it hurts. But I promise, if you hurt me, I will destroy you."

Though Ricky's words spoke of power, Ty could see the devastation in the old man's eyes. So many people came trying to hurt him, and this wound was perhaps the most painful of all.

So why, seeing the torment on Rachel's face, did Ty want to take her in his arms and tell her that everything was going to be okay? Clearly, he needed to keep his guard up now more than ever.

What was he going to do if the DNA test came back as not a match? Worse, what would he do if it was?

Chapter Four

A criminal. That was what they were treating her like. Ty's stern gaze reminded her of all the court proceedings she'd gone through with Chris. Even Ty's questions made her think he was trying to trap her into confessing to something that she didn't do.

That was the crazy thing. She hadn't done anything. But that was how the world worked. How lawyers worked.

After they left Ricky's office, Rachel went to find Katie. She hadn't intended to leave her for so long, but she also hadn't intended for her conversation with Ricky to become an inquisition. Hopefully, Leah wasn't in a hurry to leave, and she also wasn't going to judge Rachel for being a bad mother.

But when she stepped out onto the deck, she could see the children happily playing. Leah was on the dance floor with her husband, and it appeared that Janie, whom she'd been introduced to as the mother of one of the other boys, was keeping an eye on them while she chatted with the group.

Rachel walked over to where Janie was sitting. "I'm sorry it took so long. I hope Katie wasn't a bother."

If only Rachel could know whether or not Janie's smile was genuine. "It's no bother. Katie is a delight. The kids are having so much fun. We'd love it if you could join us tomorrow for church. Katie would be in the same class as the boys, and afterward, the youth group is having a water fight that the little ones can join in."

Church. She could feel Ty's gaze upon her. What was he going to do, have her burned at the stake for saying no? It was abundantly clear that these people had a strong faith, so what were they going to do when they realized that she didn't?

Janie must've sensed her hesitation. "Oh, it's safe, I promise. The teens know to watch out for the little ones, and everyone has such a great time. There is also a no-water zone, so that people who don't want to get wet don't have to."

Though Janie had completely misinterpreted Rachel's hesitation, she was glad for it. The last thing she needed was to get into a theological discussion with any of Ricky's friends, particularly the pastor's daughter.

"I don't know what we're doing tomorrow, since we're here as Ricky's guests. I wouldn't want to ruin anything they have planned."

Ty stepped beside her. "We're going to church, like always."

As Rachel looked over at him, he sent Janie a grin that would've had most women's hearts aflutter. Including Rachel's. Which was why all of this was so disturbing. Why did she have to find the absolutely worst men on the planet to be attracted to?

"My team has a whole stash of super soakers ready. We have a plan for total annihilation."

Though Rachel was sure Ty's laugh was meant to be friendly, she heard the words *total annihilation*, and she couldn't help thinking of her own situation. He was obviously a competitive man who wouldn't take losing well. What would he do when he found out he was wrong? But worse, what if there had been some kind of mix-up with the DNA website, and she was the one in the wrong?

Katie's laugh rang out from across the field where the kids were playing tag.

If Ty pressed charges, would Rachel go to jail? Would Katie end up in foster care sooner than she'd feared?

Janie laughed and said something in response to Ty, but Rachel didn't hear. Her head was pounding, throbbing, and she was starting to feel dizzy. Maybe it was stress, but maybe her kidneys were getting worse.

She looked around for a place to sit, and as she did so, Janie asked, "Are you all right, Rachel? You look flushed."

Janie scooted over and patted the bench next to her. "Sit here."

Then Janie looked up at Ty. "Go get her some water. I'm sure that like all flatlanders, she hasn't been drinking enough."

Rachel wanted to argue, because she was well aware of how much water she needed with her condition. But Ty had already turned and was walking away. And when she looked up at Janie to try to protest, Janie shook her head.

"None of that. People from Denver say all the time that they are used to the elevation, but we're at nine thousand feet, so almost four thousand feet higher, and that's quite a difference. You don't want to get altitude sickness and miss out on all the fun."

It was sweet of Janie to be concerned, and arguing with her would mean sharing everything about her health situation, which would probably be frowned upon by both Ricky and Ty. Besides, telling people you're sick—and possibly dying—was always a downer, and no one wanted to hear about it.

Ty returned with a bottle of water and handed it to her. "I saw you drink plenty earlier, but that doesn't mean you couldn't use more."

He sounded almost like he cared. Had it not been for their awkward conversation in Ricky's office, she might almost believe it.

"Always the gentleman," Janie said, smiling. Then she turned to Rachel. "But if I were you, I would steer clear of him in tomorrow's water fight if you're on the opposing team. The man is ruthless, despite his charm."

Rachel smiled back at Janie. "I've always found that the more charming a man, the more ruthless he is."

"Oh, burn," Janie said, clapping her hands. "You can probably hold your own against Ty, then, but my joking about the water fight might have given you the wrong impression. He's really a teddy bear, and I can say that with confidence, because I've known him my whole life. As long as you don't make an enemy of him, he's the best guy in the world."

Ty glared at her. "Stop. I don't know if I should run for president or run for the hills. But either way, this is a terrible conversation. I'm going to go see if Wanda has stuff to make s'mores."

"You know she does," Janie said, laughing. "And if anyone can charm them out of her, it's you."

When Ty left, Rachel looked over at Janie. "You two seem like you have a good relationship. I'd ask if he was your boyfriend, but you have Sam, and Ty said he doesn't have kids."

Janie shook her head. "He is definitely not my boyfriend. We grew up together and he's always been like an older brother to me. But since you're new here, I'm just gonna go out and say it to avoid any uncomfortable gossip. I'm not married. I never have been. Sam's father is completely out of the picture, and we prefer it that way. Yes, I know I'm the pastor's daughter. But even pastors' daughters make mistakes, and while I deeply regret a certain period of my life, I will never regret my son."

Because Rachel was such a private person, it would have never occurred to her to tell any of those things to a stranger, but she really admired Janie for it. She liked the woman's boldness and the way she owned who she was and was proud of it.

"I wouldn't regret him, either," Rachel said slowly. She didn't talk much about Katie's father or that part of her past, but Janie's confession gave her a little more strength than she usually felt. "Katie's father is dead. But we were going through a messy divorce, so I have a lot of mixed feelings about it. I don't like to talk about it much, either."

Janie put her hand over Rachel's and gave it a squeeze. "You don't have to. I'm just used to all the judgmental questions from strangers, so I like to get that information out right away."

"I don't judge," Rachel said. "I've faced too much of it in my life, and it seems to me that people's judgments of others are often completely wrong. But thank you for telling me. I'm sorry that others have made you feel like you owe them an explanation."

Janie squeezed her hand again, and even though she didn't say anything, Rachel felt like she'd found a friend. Odd, considering Rachel didn't have much experience with friends. The ones she thought she had proved to be false friends, and it hadn't felt worth the effort to try again. And yet, she'd felt that way earlier today upon meeting Della in the café, and now here, with Janie.

But it was a completely ridiculous thought. As she'd warned herself when talking with Della, she wasn't here to make friends. She was here to find a kidney. And after the situation in Ricky's office, she wasn't sure there was anything else here for her. Yes, he'd given his speech about taking care of family, but would they ever see her as that? Or would she always be the enemy who snuck her way into this place to try to ruin their lives?

When Ty arrived at the cabin the next morning, Rachel and Katie were already waiting for him on the porch.

Rachel gestured at her jeans and cotton shirt. "I hope

it's not a fancy church, because we didn't bring anything else."

Ty hated the way Rachel kept looking at him like he was her executioner. He wasn't the one who'd come to the ranch on false pretenses. He wasn't the one who had been given every opportunity to tell the truth and didn't. So why did he feel so bad about looking out for Ricky's interests?

Hoping the smile he gave them was reassuring, Ty said, "It's fine. Everyone at Columbine Springs Community Church is welcome just as they are. No fancy clothes needed." He gestured at his own Western shirt and jeans. "I don't think the Lord cares either way, as long as you're giving Him proper reverence."

Instead of looking relieved, Rachel looked more nervous. "The churches I've been to are all dress-up churches."

Ty wished he had better words of wisdom or encouragement for her, but since she looked like she thought he was going to bite her head off at any minute, she probably wouldn't find comfort in much of anything he said.

"People find our church a refreshing change. It might be unfamiliar to you, but that's okay. No one's going to judge you because you did things differently at your other church."

"I've never been to church," Katie said, jumping up. "Sam and Ryan say it's a lot of fun, and they promised to teach me all their songs and games."

Now he got it. Rachel wasn't a churchgoer, and she had the same apprehensions many people who didn't go to church had. But Pastor Roberts always made sure that people like Rachel were comfortable and felt welcomed.

"I'm sure you'll have a great time, Katie," Ty said, smiling at her and gesturing at his truck. "I saw you had a booster seat in your mom's car, so why don't you go get that out and put it in my truck? You guys are going to ride with me today."

Katie's eyes shone. "Really? I've never ridden in a big truck like that before."

He chuckled at the little girl's description. It wasn't that big of a truck. But he could imagine how a little girl not used to ranch life would see it as such.

"We can drive ourselves," Rachel said.

"Your car struggled over some of the ruts getting here. It's too much wear and tear for you to go to town, come back and then leave again. It'll save you some gas, as well. Besides, this will give me a chance to get to know you better."

By the scowl on her face, he should've left it at the wear and tear and gas. He didn't have the heart to tell her that Ricky had insisted he drive them today. Mostly because he didn't want them poking around in the ranch house with everyone at church. While they did their best to keep everything locked up, especially for the peace of mind of guests staying on the ranch, both Ty and Ricky knew that the ranch house itself didn't have the best security. They'd beefed things up with some of the crazies coming around, but until recently, Ricky had never been the kind of man to lock his doors, so he didn't always remember to keep things under lock and key. So who knew what Rachel would find available for her to snoop through?

"You mean see what secrets you can dig out of me," she said.

That, too, but he wouldn't have put it that way. "It shouldn't be a problem for you if you don't have anything to hide," he said. "If you're really family, we would naturally want to get to know you, and you would naturally want us to. That's how you build a relationship. But if you're not…"

Ty shrugged, letting her put the pieces together on her own. She wasn't stupid, and neither was he.

He gestured at the truck, where Katie was waiting outside, holding her booster seat.

"We're going to be late," he said.

Rachel followed, but she didn't look happy about it. They got the booster seat situated in the back seat of the truck, and then they were on their way.

"I need to understand something," Rachel said once they'd started down the ranch road. "You're not Ricky's family. What does your own family think of you calling him that?"

She was definitely barking up the wrong tree. "They call him family, too, as does most of this community. That's what life in a small town is about. Yes, we have our problems, but when it comes right down to it, the only way this town survives is by relying on each other, and isn't that what a family does?"

Rachel shook her head. "I wouldn't know. As I told you, I never knew my father, and my mother died when I was ten. I know my foster families did their best, but it isn't like any of them are in my life anymore, so I guess they aren't the best example, either."

The hostility in her voice hurt his heart. They hadn't

exactly brought out the fatted calf for her, but she also hadn't been honest with them, and without a DNA test, they had no reason to believe her.

But he also couldn't imagine what it must be like, going through life without the support of a family and community.

"I promise, if the DNA test comes back positive, you'll understand what family means." He wanted to say more, to tell her about how families had their ups and downs and how this one wasn't perfect, either, but he wouldn't trade it for anything. But the suspicion in her eyes told him it wouldn't do any good. Besides, he wasn't going to sell her on the family until he knew she was telling the truth.

Even then, how did he get past her deception? Family was family, but none of their relationships were based on lies.

As they continued driving, he pointed out landmarks and told them a little about the ranch, and Katie chattered excitedly, but Rachel was silent. He wished he knew what was going on in her head, but then, he also wasn't sure he wanted to know.

If she wasn't Cinco's daughter—yes, he'd threatened calling the authorities, but he wasn't sure he could do that to her little girl. For all the reasons he could think of for being a terrible human being to claim to be someone's long-lost grandchild, he could think of a million more why Katie needed her mother, and Rachel was a good one.

When they arrived at the church, some of his worries disappeared. He hadn't been exaggerating when he said this was his family—this community, these people and Ricky. But as soon as his feet landed on the walk, his mom gave him a big hug.

"Ty! You're later than usual. I heard Ricky had a gathering last night. I hope none of those cowboys got too crazy and created a fuss for you to clean up."

He gave her a squeeze, then stepped away. "No, nothing like that. Ricky has a guest he wanted me to take care of, so it took me longer to get them situated than I thought." He gestured at Rachel and Katie, who hung back. "This is Rachel Henderson, and her daughter, Katie. Rachel and Katie, this is my mom, Ann."

As he knew she would, his mom stepped forward and gave Rachel a hug. "So nice to meet you."

Rachel accepted the hug stiffly, but didn't hug back. He probably should've warned her that his mother was a hugger.

"Bob," his mom said, stepping away and waving at his father. "Come meet Ricky's guests."

His father was busy chatting with some of the other men, so his mother turned to them. "You wait right here. I'll just go get him."

When his mother was out of earshot, Rachel asked, "Does this happen with all of Ricky's guests?"

Ty shook his head. "Usually his guests are free to come and go as they please, and some come to church but others don't. The fact that Ricky had me bring you means there's something different happening here."

"Like what? She doesn't think we're romantically involved, does she?"

That would be the furthest thing from his mom's mind. While he did his best to keep his business private, most of the people in town knew that he'd been hurt enough times that he wouldn't be taking a woman hc'd just mct to church as a romantic interest. They joked that he was slower than a snail when it came to dating women, but Ty liked to be cautious. It seemed like every woman who showed an interest in him had an ulterior motive.

Was it so wrong to want to wait to get to know a person and what they were really after before getting involved?

"She knows better," he said.

Apparently, that wasn't the right answer, because Rachel scowled.

"I just met you. I wouldn't be bringing a woman I was interested in to meet my mother for the first time at church. Plus, I would have spoken about any woman I'm seeing with her prior to that meeting. So don't worry about people gossiping or thinking there's more to this than there is."

Rachel gave him another strange look, one he couldn't read. Did she think he was interested in her? Or that Ricky was trying to set them up?

"Seriously. Don't read anything into it. I'm doing Ricky a favor, that's all. I'm not interested in liars and cheats."

The startled expression on her face made him regret his last words. It was the truth, and she'd clearly proven herself to be both. But she didn't deserve the sting of the pain of his past.

And Janie, who had just walked up to them, clearly agreed. "Oh, we know all about your high sense of ethics. I don't think the perfect woman out there exists who can live up to your standards of complete and total honesty. Maybe you should give people a break."

Janie turned to Rachel. "Don't mind him. He dated this girl in college that he was going to propose to, and then he found out she was stealing his work and trying to pass it off as her own. He only found out because at first, he was the one accused of plagiarizing, and he had to prove she was the one copying off him. But ever since then, he's like a police dog when it comes to sniffing out people's lies. If your facts don't line up exactly, then that's the end of that for him."

This was why there were no secrets in small towns. But it was also why Ricky had asked him to act with discretion over the whole Rachel situation. They didn't want to out her as a liar until they had all the facts. And if she hadn't been lying about being Ricky's granddaughter, they didn't want people in this town already thinking bad things about her because of how she'd come under false pretenses.

But he also wasn't going to let Janie malign him, either. "First of all, I'm not that bad. Second, if people were just honest about things to begin with, I wouldn't need to be so suspicious. And third, the fact that I've been able to sniff out lies has saved a lot of people in this town over the years. Think about all the charlatans I've successfully chased away."

Janie groaned, then looked over at Rachel. "Sadly, he's right. That's why he's insufferable. The man is always right. And I'm not even being sarcastic."

Her face softened a little as she turned her attention

back to Ty. "But I do think that sometimes you need to give people a chance, and even though they make mistakes, you should give them the chance to make up for them. No one's perfect, not even you."

Ty could only shake his head as he tried not to laugh. This was all about the woman who'd stayed at the ranch over the winter whom he'd taken an interest in, only to find that she'd faked her injury to spend time with him. Janie had been so sure it was love, and that they were going to be together forever, if only he'd forgiven her and given her a chance. But he'd never thought of her as more than a friend.

"Or maybe I just haven't met the right person, and you should let it go. I'm sure you wouldn't like it if I took such an interest in your lack of romantic partner."

Janie groaned, as he knew she would do, but he caught a hint of a smile on Rachel's face.

"I can't imagine having such history as the two of you do," Rachel said.

The longing in her voice was evident, and he thought about some of the hints she'd dropped about her own life. He knew she lacked family but he also wondered about friends. She seemed to be uncomfortable at the closeness he had with Ricky, and how he considered Ricky family.

So what was she? Little lost girl in search of the family she never knew? Or a con artist, preying on people's sympathies?

It was especially troubling, given that she'd said she was in need of a kidney. Again, was it legitimate, or was she using it as just one more con?

Janie might have said that he was never wrong, but

in this instance, he didn't know what was right. He'd had a strong feeling that she wasn't telling the truth when they'd first met, and he'd been right. But now…he didn't know what to think or feel. Or what to believe.

Chapter Five

After she'd taken the DNA test, Ricky had invited Rachel and Katie to stay longer, but Rachel needed to get home. Not just for work, but also because she had to get back for dialysis. And yet, that plan didn't work out as she'd hoped. Her car had refused to start when they left Sunday afternoon, so Ricky had lent her one of the ranch's trucks. Which was why, Friday after work, she found herself getting into a Double R pickup truck to drive back to the Double R.

"We're going to see Mr. Ricky," Katie said, jumping up and down when Rachel picked her up from daycare.

She hated how excited her daughter was. No, *hated* wasn't the right word. But she didn't want to see the little girl disappointed. What would happen if the results said Rachel wasn't related to Ricky?

Deep in her heart, she knew that wouldn't happen. Ricky was her grandfather. But what did that mean? He couldn't give her a kidney, and it seemed pointless to develop a relationship with someone if she was just going to die anyway.

As Katie chattered on the way to the ranch, Rachel found herself distracted by those thoughts. But more than that, she also couldn't stop thinking about being in church on Sunday and the pastor's words about a relationship with Christ.

She also couldn't stop thinking of everything Ty had said about the extended family and community in Columbine Springs. Watching his interactions with Janie had made her envious in an unexpected way. And not a romantic way—it was more about the deep, close friendship that Rachel had never had before.

"Mom! You're not listening," Katie said.

Busted. "I'm sorry, I wasn't. You're right. Can you repeat that for me?"

She did her best to be honest with her daughter. To let her know that while Rachel wasn't perfect, she loved Katie with all her heart.

Was she succeeding?

She didn't know. But she hoped that if she didn't find a kidney in time, her daughter would somehow remember Rachel had done her best.

"I'm going to teach you my song I learned in Sunday school. We're going to sing it together."

Katie had been singing Bible songs ever since leaving the Sunday school classroom. Rachel didn't know who this Zacchaeus was, other than a wee little man, but Katie couldn't stop singing about him.

"Is it the Zacchaeus one?" Rachel asked.

Katie groaned. "No. My friends at school got tired of hearing it all the time, so they taught me some new songs. And now I'm going to teach you."

Her friends at school weren't the only ones, but Rachel wasn't going to say so.

"All right, let's hear it."

As Katie sang about Jesus's love and Rachel tried to learn the words, she couldn't help wondering once again if it was true. Did Jesus really love them? Was Jesus really here to save them?

Maybe on this visit she'd spend some time talking to Janie and see what insight Janie could give her. She liked the pastor's daughter, with her no-nonsense attitude and her belief that despite all of her mistakes, and all the things that seemed to have gone wrong in her life, God still loved her. Granted, Janie was a pastor's daughter, so she was probably grandfathered in on the whole God thing. But maybe, if God could see past all of Janie's mistakes, even when she should have known better, Rachel could figure out how to get God to love her, too.

Rachel had to appreciate the childlike faith in her daughter, as it made the drive go by so much more quickly. Katie's pure and sweet voice brought a peace to Rachel's heart, and even though she had no idea what her future held, she had the tiniest bit of hope.

Ty had texted her during the week to let her know that the bridge had been repaired, but he hadn't said a word about the DNA test results. She'd been tempted to ask, but she was afraid of what he might read into it. Knowing Ty and his suspicions, he'd likely think she had some sort of nefarious reason for doing so.

When she got to the ranch, things were bustling more than they had been when she was there the previous week. Ty had told her to come into the main house when she arrived, where they would sort out all the arrangements. As she walked up the steps, she quickly realized why Ty had been so put out at her showing up without a reservation.

The main lodge, with a sign that said Check-In, had a line of people going all the way out the door. Ranch hands were there, directing people where to go. It might have seemed like a rinky-dink operation from her online experience, but the activity made it clear that the Double R was a booming business.

When she entered the main ranch house, it was full of activity. More people were bustling back and forth, and Rachel almost wondered if it was the same place. But just as she was starting to look around, wondering who to ask where to go next, Ty stepped out of the hallway that led to Ricky's office.

"Good," he said. "You made it. Things are a little hectic around here, because a couple of the cabins weren't quite ready when guests started arriving earlier today. But we've got it sorted—at least I think so."

His wry grin made him look older, especially with the way his eyes crinkled at the edges, like he was trying to seem happy despite the stress.

"Is there anything I can do to help?" she asked. A dumb question, since she knew nothing about the way things operated here and probably wouldn't be able to do anything. Plus, she didn't owe him anything. It wasn't like she was obligated to help. And yet, the fatigue on his face made it impossible not to offer.

Ty shook his head. "No. Like I said, everything is under control. Let's go back and chat with Ricky. He's been expecting you."

Would it kill him to give her a hint as to what this was about? Was it the DNA test results?

As they started walking toward Ricky's office, Ty motioned to someone. Were they calling the police?

Maybe this was a bad idea.

But just as soon as they were ushered into Ricky's office and offered a seat, Wanda entered.

"Did you have a good trip?" she asked.

Rachel smiled. "Yes. Uneventful, which is the best kind."

It was so weird, making small talk when such an important thing was hanging over her.

"Good," Wanda said. "I'm going to get some refreshments ready, and Ricky has been bugging me to make more chocolate chip cookies."

Wanda looked over at Katie. "Would you like to come help?"

Now Rachel understood. Ty had been signaling to get Wanda to take Katie away.

"I'd like Katie to stay here, but thank you for your kind offer," Rachel said. She knew how this went. How many times had Chris had one of his assistants take Katie to go do something, which always somehow ended up in Rachel being declared a bad mother?

"Please," Ricky said, getting up from his desk. "We have much to discuss, adult things, and I want you to decide what's best for Katie to know before she hears anything."

And that meant what? Was she going to need to find care for her daughter while she went to jail for some imagined transgression, or had the test come back a match?

She wanted to believe that the sweet old man wasn't setting her up for something bad. But she'd also learned that if something looked too good to be true, it probably was.

"First, I need to know," she said. "Was the test positive or negative?"

Ricky looked at Ty, who nodded, then Ricky said, "Positive. Which is why we need to talk. I know you're particular about who spends time with Katie, but Wanda is good with kids, and she'll take good care of her. You've got some decisions to make, and it wouldn't be fair to get a little girl's hopes up."

Positive. The air seemed to rush out of Rachel's lungs, because even though she knew she'd been telling the truth, deep down she feared that the test she'd originally taken had been wrong.

"Mom? Are you feeling okay? You're not getting sick again, are you?" Katie's concern made Rachel feel even worse. A child shouldn't have to worry about her parent's health, constantly wonder if her mother was feeling all right. But more and more, Rachel did feel bad, tired, weak.

She turned and looked at her daughter. "Yes, sweetie. I just needed a moment to think. Would you like to go make cookies with Wanda?"

"Would I?" A wide grin filled Katie's face. "I love to bake cookies. But you never have time. When I grow up, I'm going to be a cookie baker."

Rachel gave her daughter an indulgent smile. Last week, after the firemen had visited Katie's school, she'd wanted to be a firefighter.

"Then you go have fun," Rachel said. "Ricky's right. This is a grown-up conversation."

As she waited for her daughter to leave the room, thoughts raced through Rachel's head. She told the truth the last time she'd been here. She didn't want anything from Ricky, other than the connection to someone who might be willing to donate a kidney. What else was there to discuss?

Once the door closed behind Wanda, Ricky gestured at one of the comfortable-looking chairs that she'd admired but hadn't dared sit in.

"Now that we know you're my granddaughter," Ricky said, "we have a lot to talk about."

"I'm not after your money," Rachel said. "I have a good job, and even though my medical expenses are high, I can pay for them. But like I said earlier, if you do find the grandchild you were looking for, I would appreciate being put in touch."

She could feel herself shaking as she spoke, which was ridiculous, considering she had nothing to fear. She'd told Ricky the truth, it had been confirmed and she was continuing to prove her integrity in the situation.

Ricky nodded. "I understand that. It's good to know that you're not a gold digger. But I was hoping, praying, actually, that you might give an old man the chance to be a grandfather. I made a lot of mistakes with Cinco, and it pains me to know I didn't get to see you or his other child grow up. I'd like to be part of your life. Part of Katie's life. While I can't change what happened with your mother, I'd sure like the chance to make it up right now."

Hadn't she wished for this very thing? A relationship with her grandfather? Family? It was like everything she'd ever wanted in life was dangled in front of her, except for the one thing she needed most.

"What's the catch?" she asked. All of this was too good to be true. No, he hadn't offered her anything or made her any promises, but even the fact that she'd found him and he wanted her was too much to think that this was all there was to it.

Ridiculous, considering she'd hoped he'd lead her to someone who could give her a kidney. How wild to think that she'd be okay with getting a kidney from a stranger, but not a stranger wanting to know her.

But that was the messed-up way her life worked.

And why, even though she'd like to think there was a God out there who loved her the way she and Katie had sung about the whole way here, she wasn't quite sure she could handle someone loving her like that without strings being attached.

"No catch," Ricky said. "I know you have your life to live. But I'd like you to spend some time here at the ranch, getting to know me, letting me get to know you and Katie. I've also been doing some research about kidney transplants, and while I can't guarantee that we'll find Cinco's other child, or that the child would be a match, I'd like to talk to the people in my community and see if any of them would be willing to get tested."

He'd researched kidney transplants? On one hand, it was sweet, but on the other hand, it felt a lot like the kind of control Chris had tried to exert over her. Researching things on her behalf and making decisions without consulting her.

"I saw a program on the news," Ricky continued. "This man put a sign on his truck saying he needed a kidney, and calls from all over the country came in from people willing to donate. We could do something like that for you."

She'd seen the same news program, and had briefly considered it. But things like that didn't happen for Rachel. Strangers didn't just appear out of nowhere, offering to give her a kidney.

"There's no guarantee it would work," Rachel said. "But it's nice of you to think so."

Ricky shook his head. "That is not the attitude that's going to get you a kidney. We have to think positive. No one ever got anything good out of life by thinking negative. If my kidneys weren't so old, I would give you one myself."

He turned and looked over at Ty. "You'd get tested for her, wouldn't you?"

The uncomfortable expression on Ty's face told her he would do nothing of the sort. He looked like he'd rather be drawn and quartered. Which was how a lot of people reacted. So many people didn't understand how kidney transplants worked. It was widely believed you had to die to be able to give away a kidney, but a perfectly healthy person could donate one and still lead a normal life with only one kidney.

"I'm not sure I'd want to get all cut up and go through major surgery like that," Ty said. "No offense, but what if I end up needing that extra kidney?"

That was exactly why most people weren't willing to donate a kidney.

"You've got two of them," Ricky said. "My granddaughter will die without a new kidney, so the least you could do is give her one if she needs it."

Ty looked like he was going to be sick. Although Rachel knew that any donor would go through a psychological evaluation to make sure he or she wasn't being pressured into a donation, she also didn't want someone like Ty to feel like they had to be tested.

"It's okay," Rachel said. "I'll figure something out. You don't need to make poor Ty do anything he doesn't want to do. Besides, he may not be a match."

Ricky snorted. "There is nothing poor about him. And if he wants to weasel out of it, that's fine. I already talked to the woman at the hospital in charge of transplants. She wouldn't tell me anything about what was wrong with you, because of privacy concerns, but I did convince her to come out to the ranch for a barbecue so she can talk to all the good people of this town and my guests about the benefits of kidney donation."

He did what?

Rachel stared at him. He might be her grandfather, but he'd just barely found out, and here he was already trying to control her life.

"I didn't ask you to do that." Rachel stood. "In fact, you should have asked me first. This is my personal business you're interfering in, and it's not okay for you to host some information session about kidney donation. It's not some multilevel marketing scheme—this is my life."

Ricky also stood. "And if you told me the truth the other day, without a kidney, you won't have a life. I spent a lot of time talking to that woman at the hospital about kidney donation, and a lot of lives could be saved if more people understood the benefits of donating a kidney to someone who needed it. This might not help just you, but a lot of other people."

She hadn't thought of it that way. But it still didn't make it right for Ricky to interfere.

Ty gave Ricky a look that Rachel couldn't read, but Ricky must've understood, because he sat back down. Then Ty turned to Rachel.

"I know Ricky didn't mean to invade your privacy. But when he sees a problem, he likes to solve it. Ricky might not be able to give you a kidney himself, but he knows a lot of people. Since you don't have to be related to someone to donate a kidney, one of them might be willing. You can't blame a man for looking into every option."

If she didn't know that Ty was a smooth-talking lawyer who made a living off getting people on his side, she might have been more understanding. But this wasn't about Ty trying to do the right thing or help her, it was about Ty doing his job, and somehow, that felt wrong.

"It's a lot to take in," Rachel said. "I had a long day at work today, and then the drive and now this. It's overwhelming. If you don't mind, I'd like to go to my cabin, where I can rest."

Ricky looked at Ty, who said, "Our cabins are booked for the weekend. Since you're family, you're in a guest suite here in the main house. While it doesn't have a private entrance, it does have its own sitting room, a bedroom and a bathroom. You'll take your meals in the dining room, and hopefully it will give you and Ricky a chance to get to know one another better."

Once again, it felt like she was being forced into a position she didn't want to be in. From her earlier visit, she knew there were no hotels nearby, and if all the cabins were booked, she had no place else to go.

"And if I don't like that arrangement?" she asked.

Ty sighed, like she was being difficult. And maybe she was, but her life had just been completely upended, and too much was being thrown at her at once.

"You can have my cabin," Ty said. "It'll take me an hour or so to straighten up and get the things I need, but I can stay here at Ricky's instead. We weren't trying to make you uncomfortable, but to let you know that you are part of this family, and that you're welcome."

Now she did feel like she was being difficult. The pained expression on Ricky's face and the return of the lines in Ty's brow told her that they were doing their best to make this a good experience for her.

She also had to admit, it was kind of Ty to offer to give up his own cabin to make her feel more comfortable.

"I'll be fine here at the house," she said. "I don't want to put anyone out. But can't you see how difficult this is to take everything in all at once? You've had all this time after you found out the results were positive to make plans, but I haven't. Now suddenly you want me to stay in the main house, you're organizing an information session to get people to donate a kidney to me, and who knows what else you're going to take over in my life? I had everything under control until you stepped in."

Ty nodded slowly. "Everything except the kidney you need. I'm sorry if it seems like we've overstepped, but family helps each other. That's what community does, too. When one of us has a need, everyone steps in to fill that need. Not everyone here will be willing or able to donate a kidney, but if you don't ask, the answer will always be no. And you never know—someone here just might say yes."

His motivational speech might have meant a little something more if he hadn't looked so terrified at the prospect of donating a kidney to her. He'd be asking others to do something he wasn't willing to do himself. And yet she didn't blame him for being unwilling. If she were in his shoes, she wouldn't be jumping up and down to give a kidney to a stranger.

Maybe that was why they hadn't yet found a donor for her. Because if she were completely honest, until her own illness, she would have never considered helping someone in this way. It wasn't completely unreasonable for someone to be unwilling to help.

Still, this wasn't about her. It was, in the sense of her life being on the line. But really, this was about Katie, and making sure Katie had a mother and didn't grow up in foster care.

"All right," she said. "I guess we can do this community event about kidney awareness. I'm not one to ask for help from strangers, but given that I'm running out of time, I'm willing to do just about anything."

As the men looked at each other and nodded, Rachel hoped that agreeing to all this nonsense wasn't a terrible mistake.

Talk about difficult. Ty had never run into someone so obstinate in his life. The woman would die without a kidney, but rather than being grateful for their help, she acted as though they were trying to hasten her end.

"I promise we'll do everything we can to keep it low-key," Ty said. "But that brings me to the next item we need to discuss. Ricky would like to announce that you're his granddaughter. Are you okay with that?"

The length of her hesitation made Ty regret his suspicions of her. So far, after all of Ricky's generosity and acknowledgment, rather than being excited about it, Rachel seemed withdrawn, like this was the last thing she wanted. All this time he'd been trying to protect Ricky from a gold digger, and this woman didn't seem to want to have anything to do with him.

But that was also probably Ty's fault.

He'd done nothing to make Rachel feel comfortable or welcome up to this point. He couldn't blame her for being apprehensive about him or Ricky. Which meant he'd have to do more to make up for his previous treatment toward her.

Yet, it also didn't erase the fact that she'd been so deceptive when they'd first met. If she'd just told the truth up front, he still would have been suspicious, but they'd have taken the test and there wouldn't be all the bad feelings between them. That was why he hated lies and deception so much. You could plug up a hole in a board, but the scar would always be there.

"You don't have to make a decision now," Ricky said, looking nervously at Ty as he tried to fill the uncomfortable silence.

"That's right," Ty said. "It's up to you if and when you tell people who you are in relation to Ricky. What's more important is that we make your need for a kidney known, and hopefully, someone will be willing to step up."

Rachel gave him a hard look. "Step up? You make it sound like paying child support, not donating a vital organ. This is a big deal, and even you aren't willing to do it. You can't simplify it like that. We'll present the information, and if someone is willing to sacrifice, then fine. Otherwise, that's fine, too."

If he'd been closer to Ricky, Ricky would have probably kicked him. Saying he wasn't willing to donate a kidney hadn't been the brightest move on Ty's part. But he also couldn't lie and say the thought of being cut open didn't creep him out a bit. Okay, a lot. He'd never been into blood and needles, which was why he'd become a lawyer and not a doctor. Besides, why would he risk his own health and safety for someone who was so deceptive? Yes, she was Ricky's granddaughter. Which meant he'd be nice to her. But sacrifice a kidney?

Not for someone like her.

"I'm sorry, you're right," Ty said. "I'm not comfortable with stuff like this, but I'm sure someone else is, and we can keep praying that someone out there is willing to help you. I'll do everything I can to support that endeavor."

The resigned look on Rachel's face told him he hadn't quite fixed things. But he also wasn't ready to give her a pass for how she'd deceived them.

"I don't know what to do," she said, sighing. "I came here looking for a donor, not a family. But I understand that things are done differently here. Why don't you show me to my room and give me a chance to rest? I'll think about what I want in terms of being known as Ricky's granddaughter, and I'll let you know my decision when I'm ready."

Ty hated the pain in Ricky's eyes, but he could also see the exhaustion in Rachel's. Though her doctor wouldn't give any information on Rachel's condition, both he and Ricky had researched what they could piece together, and fatigue was a normal symptom Rachel would be feeling. It made him feel bad about how tired she'd been on her last visit, and all the ways he'd pushed her when she probably just needed some rest.

If only Janie could see him now, being sympathetic to Rachel, even when he was upset with her for how she'd acted.

"That sounds fine," Ty said. "Take all the time you need. I'll show you to your room, and then I'll bring up your bags. You rest. Let Katie enjoy her time with Wanda."

For a moment he was afraid she was going to refuse, but then she nodded. "Are you sure Katie won't be a bother?"

Ricky cackled as he pounded on his desk. "You're making Wanda's dreams come true. Those kids of hers aren't getting any closer to providing her with grandchildren, and her grandma biological clock is ticking so loud, it's like a time bomb. You don't know how desperate this house is to have a child in it again."

At his words, a faint smile crossed Rachel's face, but it made the exhaustion there all the more evident.

"All right," she said, sounding defeated.

Ty led her out of the office and up the stairs to the guest suite. He'd stayed there once when his cabin had flooded due to a frozen pipe breaking, and he'd found it comfortable. Knowing Wanda, she'd probably also added some special touches to make it feel like home for Rachel and Katie.

While they wouldn't go public with the information about Rachel, they had told Wanda, since she was practically family and she'd been running the house for years.

As Ty escorted her upstairs, he could sense her apprehension. What was he supposed to say that would make her feel better? What *could* he say?

"I just wanted to tell you," he began, "I'm sorry if I was a bit rough on you the last time you were here. You need to understand that we've had a lot of people trying to cheat Ricky out of his money. I was torn because you seemed like a good person, but you'd be amazed at the masks people put on if they think they can trick you into getting what they want."

As far as apologies went, it wasn't perfect. And Ty knew it. But he also didn't think she deserved the full apology. He hadn't been the one to lie. Anyone would be hesitant to apologize to a liar.

But Ricky had told him to make things right. Rachel and Katie were Ricky's only connection to Cinco, and for Ricky's sake, Ty had to try to forgive Rachel for her deception.

When Rachel didn't answer, he said, "I usually do a better job with words. Most people think my speech is flawless, especially in the courtroom. But in this case, I guess I don't know what to say. I was wrong, but I'd like to think I did it for the right reasons."

Still nothing. Rachel continued looking at him like she thought he was a jerk. If it weren't for Ricky, Ty would have given up already. As far as Ty was concerned, he didn't need a relationship with someone like her. But Ricky did. Which meant Ty would go the extra mile.

"I hope you'll find it in your heart to give me a second chance," Ty said as they reached the landing. He gestured at the first door on the right. "This is you."

He pulled a key out of his pocket and handed it to her. "I know we said you're part of the family now, and you are. We don't usually have guests come into this wing, and you should be safe. But just in case you needed a little peace of mind, I had a lock put on the door so you can lock it as you please."

She took the key and stared at it. "You had it installed?"

He shrugged. "After everything that's happened, you don't have a reason to trust us. Even though we welcome you as family, it might still feel like you're staying with strangers. This is one more way to make you feel secure."

After unlocking the door, Ty pointed out the layout of the wing, including where Wanda stayed as well as the hallway leading to the wing that housed Ricky's quarters. As they entered the suite, he watched as she took in all the details. The sitting area had a wet bar, and Wanda had put together a small tray of refreshments.

When he saw her gaze go that way, he said, "The fridge is stocked with some things Wanda thought you might like."

"You must think I'm incredibly ungrateful," she said. "You have to understand. I'm not used to people rolling out the red carpet for me."

As he looked at the tiny lines around her eyes, he could see the strain and the toll dealing with her situation all alone must've taken on her. The preliminary report from his investigator indicated that everything she'd said was true. But other information had also come to light. Katie's father had been a well-known lawyer, his name familiar to Ty. Ty hadn't liked him much, because the man was a hothead. Chris Henderson was a good lawyer, and given the custody battle with Rachel at the time of his death, Ty felt sorry for Rachel. Chris wasn't the sort of man to give up without a fight, and he played dirty tricks. The investigator had indicated Chris was having Rachel investigated for being an unfit mother. Ty hadn't spent much time with Rachel, but he already knew it couldn't be true. Still, he would look into the allegations, if only to be thorough and give everyone peace of mind.

But for now he had to work on making Rachel feel comfortable here.

"We're trying not to overwhelm you too much," Ty said, looking at the expression on her face and trying to read it. If he had to hazard a guess, he'd say that their attempts had failed. She looked more than overwhelmed, and he wished he could do something about it.

"I know," Rachel said. "And I appreciate that. I'm sure my coming on the scene wasn't what you were expecting, either. You asked me for a second chance. We could both use a fresh start. Let's just pretend we're meeting for the first time today."

The tired smile she gave him told him that what she needed wasn't another half-sincere apology, but time.

Something she might not have much of, if they weren't successful in finding her a kidney.

And there was still the other matter. Of wanting to hug her and tell her it was going to be okay, and that they'd get through it together. Which was something Ty wouldn't do, no matter how tempting. He couldn't be that man for her, not when she'd already shown him that when their desires were at odds, she wouldn't hesitate to do anything to get what she wanted—including lie.

People might call Ty ruthless, but there were lines he'd never cross. He deserved a woman who adhered to those same principles.

"Fine," Ty said. "I'm Ty Warner. Welcome to the Double R Ranch."

He extended a hand and gave her the same warm welcome he'd give any other guest. She might be someone special to Ricky, but beyond that, to Ty, she was just like anyone else, and he wasn't going to let himself get attached.

Chapter Six

As soon as Rachel got out of the car at church on Sunday and let Katie out, Katie went running to where her new friends, Sam and Ryan, were gathered with a bunch of other children. Her heart melted a little bit as Sam gave her a hug when she handed him the picture she'd painstakingly drawn for him earlier in the week. She had another for Ryan, who also hugged her when she gave him the picture. It was weird to Rachel, finding herself a member of this community and being welcomed with open arms.

She cast a glance over at Ricky, who was talking with Ty and the pastor. Even though it went against her better judgment, she'd agreed to allow him to let people quietly know that she was his granddaughter, and, as much as she hated to impose on a bunch of strangers, that she was in need of a kidney. From the way they all turned and looked at her, that must have been what they were talking about.

It didn't make sense, how she'd been willing to approach a stranger because she thought him a long-lost relative capable of connecting her with someone who would give her a kidney and yet the thought of having these complete strangers aware of her situation seemed, well, uncomfortable. She'd always earned her way through life, so to simply ask someone felt wrong. Like she was taking something without being deserving of it.

Janie approached her. "I'm so glad you're back. Even though we just met, I've come to think of you as a friend. I know that sounds weird, and I'm probably coming off as some creepy desperate pastor's daughter, but I really enjoyed talking to you, and it's been fun seeing how quickly our kids made friends."

It was a little weird and awkward, but that was what she liked about Janie. Even though she was the pastor's daughter, she seemed human, and the fact that Janie didn't have it all together gave her hope that maybe Rachel didn't have to, either.

"It's fine," Rachel said. "I enjoyed talking to you, as well. I'm not used to having a lot of friends. Even though I live in Denver, I hope I will be coming here more."

"You are?" Janie's smile lit her eyes, and it was kind of nice to think that maybe she did have a new friend. Not that she would get attached to the idea, because she'd had friends, lots of them, or at least that was what she'd thought until her nightmare with Chris had begun.

"Are you going to do a marketing campaign for them? I don't mean to sound nosy, but I heard Ty talking about it, and he seemed very excited about your ideas."

He did? That was news to her, but she and Ty hadn't had time to talk about her marketing plans. She got the sense that Ty still didn't fully trust her. He'd been welcoming enough, more than enough, actually. But sometimes there was something in the way he looked at her that made her feel like he still wasn't sure about her.

"Actually, we haven't talked about it," Rachel said. "I put together a small presentation for Ricky, but he hasn't seen it. I think I can do some good for the Double R, but of course, that's up to Ricky."

Janie leaned in. "Well, considering the way Ty looks at you, I have a feeling you could present scribbles on a piece of paper, and they'd still be interested."

Rachel stared at her new friend. "That's ridiculous. First of all, Ty seems to have the kind of integrity that wouldn't be swayed by his personal feelings for someone. But more than that, I don't think he likes me very much at all."

Janie snickered. "That's what he wants you to think. What he wants everyone to think. But I know Ty. He likes you. I think he's just been looking for the right person."

Well, this was awkward. True, it was flattering to know that Ty may be interested. But there were so many reasons why Rachel absolutely could not get involved with him, the least of which being that she didn't know if she'd be around tomorrow. And then there was the fact of his profession. He'd do anything to win. That was something she had to remember whenever she was tempted to let her guard down around him.

Men like him were never interested in the truth.

She couldn't say any of this to Janie. Instead, she smiled at her new friend. "That's sweet of you to say, but I think Ty is just looking out for me because of Ricky. Nothing more, nothing less."

Her words didn't wipe the grin from Janie's face. "If that's what you want to tell yourself. I get it. Being a single mom is hard, and opening your heart to romance again is even harder. But Ty is a good guy, and I would recommend him to just about anyone."

Rachel stared at her friend. "Does that mean you are open to romance?"

"The concept, yes." Janie shrugged. "The reality? Absolutely not. I grew up with all the guys in this town. I know them. All their secrets, and all the reasons why they're not right for me. But just because I'm not suited for any of them doesn't mean I can't see when someone else is."

The church bell rang, preventing Rachel from responding. Maybe that was best. She didn't want to get in some weird argument with the first person to befriend her in a long time.

As they walked into church, Rachel saw Ty talking to his parents. She'd briefly met them the last time she'd been to church. Ty had told her that everyone in the community considered one another family, but the way Ty let his mom hug him tight told her that he shared an even deeper love with his parents. A pang of envy hit her. What would it be like to have such close relationships?

Janie grabbed her arm. "You should sit with me today."

Then she turned in the direction of the kids, who were already running toward her. "Let's get you guys checked in for Sunday school."

The feeling in Rachel's stomach resembled how she felt when she was getting ready to ride a roller coaster, and it hadn't started yet, but she knew what was coming. Last week she'd sat with Ty and Ricky because she'd been forced to. Or at least it had felt that way to her. But here, Janie had taken her arm because she wanted to.

Ty stepped in beside them. "You're sitting with us, right?" he asked.

"Actually, I was thinking of sitting with Janie," she said.

Ricky joined them. "That's a fine idea. I like that you're making friends here. Gives you more ties to the community. More reasons to come back."

Then Ricky grinned at Janie. "You're never going to believe this. Cinco had more than one kid. Rachel's my long-lost granddaughter."

Janie's eyes widened as she looked over at Rachel. Confusion and disappointment filled her face. "Why didn't you say anything? I thought we were friends. Why wouldn't you tell me about Ricky?"

Before Rachel could answer, Janie turned and grabbed Sam's hand. "Let's get you signed in to your class."

The look Ty gave Rachel made it clear. Once again she'd messed up and violated some code that he held sacred. Okay, fine. She hadn't told Janie about Ricky or her kidneys, or about much of anything. But she was new at this friend thing. The last friends she'd had sold her out to Chris and his lies. Not one of them had stood beside her. So why should she be expected to be open with these people she barely knew?

A tiny voice whispered that maybe she should tell Janie just that. Maybe she should let go of the armor she'd carried based on her past wounds, because otherwise, she would end up alone.

Was that what people meant when they said God was talking to them? And why was God finally showing up in her life now?

But she had to admit, the voice had a point. She'd heard Ricky speak of his regret in pushing his son away, and how he didn't want to spend the rest of his days alone. She'd thought Ricky ridiculous for thinking that, considering so many people loved him.

No one loved her like that, except for Katie.

So maybe it was time for her to give it a chance.

And that was why Ty didn't trust liars. Did Rachel realize how much it meant that Janie had been willing to trust her as a friend? Janie had tons of acquaintances, and everyone liked her. But he hadn't seen Janie connect with someone like this in a long time. And Rachel had ruined it with her lies.

As Ty shook his head, Ricky nudged him. Everyone was standing for the opening hymn, and here he was, sitting there woolgathering like an idiot.

It shouldn't matter if Rachel hurt Janie's feelings, other than the fact that Janie was a good friend. But it was more than that. It served as confirmation that he couldn't trust Rachel to...

What?

What exactly did he think he needed to trust Rachel for anyway?

It would be easier if they weren't reciting the Lord's

"One Minute" Survey

You get up to **FOUR** books <u>and</u> Mystery Gifts...

ABSOLUTELY FREE!

Romance

YOU pick your books – WE pay for everything!

Suspense

See inside for details.

YOU pick your books –
WE pay for everything.
You get up to FOUR new books and TWO Mystery Gifts..
absolutely FREE!
Total retail value: Over $20!

Dear Reader,

Your opinions are important to us. So if you'll participate in our fast and free "One Minute" Survey, **YOU** can pick up to four wonderful books that **WE** pay for!

As a leading publisher of women's fiction, we'd love to hear from you. That's why we promise to reward you for completing our survey.

IMPORTANT: Please complete the survey and return it. We'll send your Free Books and Free Mystery Gifts right away. **And we pay for shipping and handling too!** ← *We pay for EVERYTHING!*

Try **Love Inspired® Romance Larger-Print** books and fall in love with inspirational romances that take you on an uplifting journey of faith, forgiveness and hope.

Try **Love Inspired® Suspense Larger-Print** books where courage and optimism unite in stories of faith and love in the face of danger

Or TRY BOTH!

Thank you again for participating in our "One Minute" Survey. It really takes just a minute (or less) to complete the survey… and your free books and gifts will be well worth it!

Sincerely,

Pam Powers

Pam Powers
for Reader Service

"One Minute" Survey

GET YOUR FREE BOOKS AND FREE GIFTS!

✓ Complete this Survey   ✓ Return this survey

DETACH AND MAIL CARD TODAY!

1 Do you try to find time to read every day?
☐ YES   ☐ NO

2 Do you prefer books which reflect Christian values?
☐ YES   ☐ NO

3 Do you enjoy having books delivered to your home?
☐ YES   ☐ NO

4 Do you find a Larger Print size easier on your eyes?
☐ YES   ☐ NO

YES! I have completed the above "One Minute" Survey. Please send me my Free Books and Free Mystery Gifts (worth over $20 retail). I understand that I am under no obligation to buy anything, as explained on the back of this card.

☐ I prefer Love Inspired® Romance Larger Print 122/322 IDL GNTG

☐ I prefer Love Inspired® Suspense Larger Print 107/307 IDL GNTG

☐ I prefer BOTH 122/322 & 107/307 IDL GNTS

FIRST NAME   LAST NAME

ADDRESS

APT.#   CITY

STATE/PROV.   ZIP/POSTAL CODE

© 2019 HARLEQUIN ENTERPRISES ULC
™ and ® are trademarks owned by Harlequin Enterprises ULC. Printed in the U.S.A.

Offer limited to one per household and not applicable to series that subscriber is currently receiving.
Your Privacy—The Reader Service is committed to protecting your privacy. Our Privacy Policy is available online at www.ReaderService.com or upon request from the Reader Service. We make a portion of our mailing list available to reputable third parties that offer products we believe may interest you. If you prefer that we not exchange your name with third parties, or if you wish to clarify or modify your communication preferences, please visit us at www.ReaderService.com/consumerschoice or write to us at Reader Service Preference Service, P.O. Box 9062, Buffalo, NY 14240-9062. Include your complete name and address.
LI/SLI-520-OM20

READER SERVICE—Here's how it works:

Accepting your 2 free books and 2 free gifts (gifts valued at approximately $10.00 retail) places you under no obligation to buy anything. You may keep the books and gifts and return the shipping statement marked "cancel." If you do not cancel, approximately one month later we'll send you 6 more books from each series you have chosen, and bill you at our low, subscribers-only discount price. Love Inspired® Romance Larger-Print books and Love Inspired® Suspense Larger-Print books consist of 6 books each month and cost just $5.99 each in the U.S. or $6.24 each in Canada. That is a savings of at least 17% off the cover price. It's quite a bargain! Shipping and handling is just 50¢ per book in the U.S. and $1.25 per book in Canada*. You may return any shipment at our expense and cancel at any time — or you may continue to receive monthly shipments at our low, subscribers-only discount price plus shipping and handling. *Terms and prices subject to change without notice. Prices do not include sales taxes which will be charged (if applicable) based on your state or country of residence. Canadian residents will be charged applicable taxes. Offer not valid in Quebec. Books received may not be as shown. All orders subject to approval. Credit or debit balances in a customer's account(s) may be offset by any other outstanding balance owed by or to the customer. Please allow 3 to 4 weeks for delivery. Offer available while quantities last.

▼ If offer card is missing write to: Reader Service, P.O. Box 1341, Buffalo, NY 14240-8531 or visit www.ReaderService.com ▼

BUSINESS REPLY MAIL
FIRST-CLASS MAIL   PERMIT NO. 717   BUFFALO, NY

POSTAGE WILL BE PAID BY ADDRESSEE

READER SERVICE
PO BOX 1341
BUFFALO NY 14240-8571

NO POSTAGE
NECESSARY
IF MAILED
IN THE
UNITED STATES

Prayer, asking God to forgive their debts as they forgive their debtors.

Holding a grudge against Rachel was wrong. Ty knew that. But what was the difference between holding a grudge against someone and being wary of them based on their past, and seemingly present, actions?

Father, help me.

It was all Ty could pray, under the circumstances. Especially as he glanced over at Rachel, who was singing along like something in her heart had changed. The last time they'd been here, she'd acted wary, mistrustful. But now she seemed open to what God had to say.

That was another reason why, even though he had moments of liking her and wondering what if, he couldn't follow that trail of thought. Janie might mock Ty for his standards, but they were God's standards, and he wanted a woman in his life who was willing to live according to them. That was why he had no respect for Rachel's ex. Yes, Chris had been known as a good lawyer, but he'd do anything to win. Ty was also a good lawyer, but he'd never compromised his beliefs for anyone or anything.

At the end of the service, Pastor Roberts called Ricky up for his announcement. The pastor had graciously agreed to let Ricky tell the congregation about Rachel and invite everyone to the barbecue tonight to explain about Rachel's condition. When Ricky talked about Rachel needing a kidney, Pastor Roberts held out a hand.

"I know we're technically done with church, and some of you have things to do, so you're excused. But

Rachel, if you wouldn't mind coming up here, I think we all need to pray for you."

Rachel had ended up sitting with them since Janie had been so cold to her. Ty could tell from the expression on Rachel's face that no one had offered prayer over her like this before. Just like the enthusiastic welcome they'd tried to give her at the ranch, this was overwhelming for her.

He took her hand and squeezed. "It's okay. I'll come up with you," he said quietly. "Some other people will follow, and we're going to pray for you. We just want to share God's love with you."

Rachel looked up at him and nodded.

When they walked over to Pastor Roberts, Ty wasn't surprised at all the people who followed. Janie was one of the first who joined them.

"I'm sorry I was so snippy with you," Janie said quietly as they were walking up. She took Rachel's other hand. "You've got way more on your mind than telling your life story to someone you just met. I guess I got carried away with meeting a new friend."

Ty's heart softened as Rachel looked over at her. "It's okay. I haven't had a friend in so long, I'm probably rusty at being one myself. We'll figure it out together."

Her words shamed him. In truth, Ty was also rusty at making friends. And at letting a new person into his life. He'd been so busy protecting himself, protecting Ricky, that he wasn't so good at opening up, either. It wasn't like he'd told Rachel everything about him. So why did he and everyone else expect it of her? Was he wrong for not letting her tell everyone her business in her own time?

When Pastor Roberts started to pray, Ty could feel the love and support of everyone in the community praying with them. He'd had this love and support his whole life.

All this time he'd never considered what it meant to walk in someone else's shoes, but after Pastor Roberts's sermon on the topic, Ty was determined to do a better job of it. He wouldn't fully trust Rachel, but he'd try. Things would be better when he had the full report from the investigator, and maybe Ty would follow up on a few things of his own.

He glanced at Janie, whose apology had made him feel bad. Even though Janie had been deeply wounded in the past, she was still open to loving and caring for others. That openness didn't apply to dating, however, and he wasn't sure he blamed her.

Which was why Ty wasn't sure how he was supposed to give Rachel another chance. Technically, yes, that was what the Bible said he should do. He was working on forgiving her, but he didn't know how.

It seemed like the more time he spent with her, the more he found himself liking her.

Like now.

Though she wasn't fully committed to Christ, she'd been willing to keep coming to church, to let a bunch of strangers pray for her, and whether she realized it or not, to let God work in her heart. Because Ty had always known and loved God, he didn't know what it must be like for Rachel, having all this thrown at her at once.

When everyone finished praying for Rachel, Ty felt a greater peace about the situation than he'd known prior.

He didn't have any answers, but he did know that God had it under control.

As the crowd thinned out, Rachel turned to Ty and hugged him.

"Thank you for giving me a chance, even though you aren't sure about me." Tears shone in her eyes. "I don't know if I'll get a new kidney or not. But after today I do know that God loves me. Thank you for encouraging me to come up here, because otherwise, I'd have been too scared."

Then she turned to Janie. "You know what your dad said about accepting Christ? I think I need you to talk to me more about that."

The smile on Janie's face almost made it all worthwhile. God worked in many mysterious ways, and if He could use the messed-up way Rachel came into their lives to bring Rachel into their fold, then maybe Ty needed to do more to figure out what having Rachel here meant for him personally.

"I would love that," Janie said, giving Rachel a squeeze before turning her attention on Ty. "Go get the kids from Sunday school and keep them occupied. My mom is teaching their class today, so if you tell her I had to take Rachel to get a jelly doughnut, she'll let you take them."

"Your mom came to church today? I thought the chemo was making her too sick to come," Ty said, trying not to sound overly concerned. He was one of the few people in the church who knew just how sick Janie's mom was.

"Yes," Janie said. "So don't let her tire herself out

by staying late for some kids whose moms are getting right with Jesus."

He chuckled as he shook his head slowly.

Janie gave him a stern look. "Be sure you mention the jelly doughnuts. That's our code word to let someone who's not me pick the kids up. The other volunteers wouldn't do it, but my mom understands."

That was what Ty loved about their community. The trust they'd all built.

Maybe Rachel had never had that, so maybe she didn't understand just how important it was to be open with the people around you.

When he got to the classroom, Sam and Katie were the last two in there. Janie's mom looked thinner and more exhausted than he'd ever seen her.

"Hey, Mama R. Janie told me to tell you that she and Rachel had to get some jelly doughnuts, so I should pick the kids up."

Janie's mom gave him a weary smile. "I'm so glad. Janie does love her jelly doughnuts. I always thought she'd follow in Jeff's footsteps and lead the church, but…" She shook her head. "Ah, well, we all serve the Lord in our own ways."

Pastor Roberts poked his head into the room. "Are you about ready to head home, Bette?"

She nodded slowly. "Today wore me out more than I thought it would. I just thought that if I could be doing what I loved, spending time with the children, I'd feel better."

The tender look that passed between the couple put an ache in Ty's heart. He'd be lying if he said he didn't want that kind of love for himself. Janie said his standards were too high and that he was too picky.

"Where's Janie?" Pastor Roberts asked, looking around the room.

His wife gave him a smile that spoke of pride, but must have taken a great deal of effort. "Getting jelly doughnuts with Rachel."

Pastor Roberts nodded. "I thought there might be something happening in Rachel's heart. The poor woman. So much to deal with. It's good that she's letting the Lord help her with it."

"What's with the jelly doughnuts?" Ty asked.

A wide grin filled the pastor's face. "They were her favorite when she was little. Praying with people is her favorite thing as an adult, so we made that our code for when Janie's running behind. That way, no one is called out or made to feel uncomfortable. And it keeps our little Sam safe."

At the mention of Sam's name, he got up from what he was playing with and came running. "Poppa!"

Katie also got up and came to them, looking hesitant. Then Sam nudged her. "Poppa, you have to be Katie's poppa, too. She doesn't have a dad, just like me. And since she doesn't have a poppa, either, I told her that I would share you."

When Pastor Roberts squatted down to hug the children, tears pricked the backs of Ty's eyes. Even though his anger and frustration had been directed at Rachel, he hadn't thought about what things must be like for Katie.

Katie had no family, other than Rachel and Ricky, but they hadn't yet told Katie. They'd probably have to soon, since everyone knew now, but Rachel had said she needed to do it in her own time and her own way.

What would happen to Katie if Rachel died?

While Ty wasn't sure he could risk one of his own kidneys, he would pray for someone else to be willing to do the same. But that felt like a cop-out. Even though he thought he had all the information, he would listen prayerfully to the presentation about kidney donation to see what God put on his heart.

After they all said their goodbyes to the pastor and his wife, Ty decided to let the kids continue playing, since they'd seemed to be having fun with the dollhouse.

"Ty!" Sam said, gesturing at them. "Come play with us."

He joined them on the floor, and Sam grabbed a boy doll that had been tossed aside. "You can be him," Sam said. "We usually just play mommies, since we don't have dads, but it will be good to have a dad."

Then Sam gave an awkward shrug. "You don't have kids, though, so you can't be a dad. Maybe you could be the neighbor."

That was what he'd always been. The neighbor. The friend. But never the dad. Which was something he'd like to be. Funny how a child could put it all in perspective.

"I wish I had a dad," Katie said quietly. "One who would take me fishing and hiking and swimming."

She looked up at Ty, hope shining in her eyes.

It was like a knife to his heart. How was he supposed to tell a kid that he'd love to be her dad, but he wasn't sure he could trust her mom enough to fall in love with her?

Sam saved him from having to answer. "I pray for God to bring me a dad every day." He looked up at Ty. "I already asked Mom if you could be my dad, but she said no way."

"But I want him to be my dad," Katie said, her brow crumpling.

Who knew he'd be the popular choice among kids? Even though he'd known Sam his whole life, it was Katie's plea that tugged at Ty's heart the most. And yet, he couldn't say yes.

"I love you both," Ty said, putting his arms around them. "But being someone's dad means being someone's husband. I can't do that for your moms. But what I can do is promise that I will always be there for you, no matter what."

Both kids snuggled up to him, and it was the best feeling in the world. If only he could tell them how desperately he'd love to be a dad.

Then Sam pulled away. "I have a soccer game on Wednesday."

"I'll be there," Ty said. Janie had given Ty the schedule and he came to a lot of Sam's games.

Katie gave him a pout. "I don't play soccer."

"I'll still be there for whatever you need. Anytime you need me, you call, okay?" It seemed like a weird thing to say to a little kid, but he wanted to give Katie some kind of reassurance.

"But I don't know your number," Katie said.

Ty pulled his business card out of his pocket and handed it to her. "Now you do."

She held it against her cheek like it was a prized possession. Sam glared at him. "You never gave me one of those."

Ugh. The kids weren't even close to siblings, but they still had a rivalry going.

"You have my number memorized already. But just so you're not left out, here you go." He gave Sam a card, then Sam jumped up and ran to the door.

"Mom! Look what Ty gave me!"

Katie also jumped up. "And me!"

Rachel was standing next to Janie, and he wondered how much they'd heard. From the annoyed look on Janie's face, probably a lot. Sam was constantly begging Ty to be his dad, and both Ty and Janie were in agreement that it was never, ever, ever going to happen. While they both dearly loved one another as friends, they had never had any romantic feelings about each other.

Rachel, on the other hand...

Ty shook his head. Not going to go there.

"We've got to get going, buddy. We're bringing lunch to Gramma and Poppa," Janie said. Then she looked over at Ty. "And I will call you later."

A threat. But he wasn't worried. They'd had this conversation a hundred times before, and probably would a thousand more. He wasn't supposed to encourage Sam in his dad fantasies, but he didn't know what else to do. The boy needed a man to love him, and Ty did.

"Did you get everything worked out?" Ty asked Rachel.

She nodded and held up a Bible. "Janie gave me a list of some things to read." Then she looked down at Katie. "You and I will also need to talk later."

Considering she didn't like how they'd already interfered in her life, and how protective she was of Katie, she'd probably read him the riot act over how he'd stepped in with Katie. But what else was he supposed to do? He might not have known Katie long, but he could already say that he loved the little girl, and would do just as much for her as he'd done for Sam.

At least he'd have some time to get his thoughts together. Katie had already started chattering their ears off about what they'd done in Sunday school. Hopefully, he could find a way to convey his commitment to Katie without making Rachel think he was offering anything that crossed a line.

But as Rachel laughed at Katie's retelling of how one of the boys stuck a crayon up his nose, Ty's heart did a funny little flip-flop. There was so much to like about Rachel. And were it not for the way she'd deceived them about her intentions, he might have been willing to ask her on a date to find out if the chemistry he felt meant anything. Instead, he ignored the twinge he felt as she laughed again, brushing back her hair, tempting him to think about wanting more.

Chapter Seven

Had Katie really asked Ty to be her dad? The scene played over in Rachel's mind as she drove to work after her weekend at the ranch. She hadn't had any alone time to process, though she'd admit that as a single mom, alone time was often hard to come by. Ty had handled it beautifully, at least until he'd promised her he'd always be there for her. He had no right to make her such promises. Especially when Rachel couldn't even make them herself.

She'd briefly considered talking to Ricky to see if he would be willing to take guardianship if Rachel died. But he was an old man, and who knew how many good years he had ahead of him? At his age, she couldn't saddle him with such a young child, even though they adored one another.

She'd thought about asking Ty for his legal opinion, but she also wasn't sure she was ready to let herself be that vulnerable with him.

And yet, as she thought of how he'd so lovingly taken

the kids into his arms and promised to always be there for them, her heart just melted.

For a moment she'd almost allowed herself to believe that Ty could help them. But how did she know whether he was sincere in what he'd told the children, or if he was just telling them what they wanted to hear? Lawyers were good at that, which was why she was hesitant to seek out legal advice from him. But her last visit with the doctor hadn't been good. She needed a kidney, and soon. Hopefully, with yesterday's barbecue…

She had to admit that everyone was so welcoming and kind. Ricky had said the turnout would be good, because their community would support one of their own. Rachel hadn't expected the crowd to be larger than the one that had shown up for Ricky's impromptu band tryout. Even more surprisingly, a lot of people had signed up on the list for more information.

But just because people signed up on a list to get more information on becoming a living donor didn't mean they would be a match or willing to go under the knife.

Rachel sighed. It didn't do any good to have false hope. Even if she got a kidney, there was no guarantee her body wouldn't reject it or there wouldn't be complications on the operating table. Whether she liked it or not, she should talk to a lawyer.

But could she trust Ty?

The office was quiet when she got in—not surprising, since it was usually just her and her boss, Dan, who opened the office. They both liked the quiet time before everyone else got in and they were officially open for business. Immediately after she set her bag on her desk, Dan came into her office.

"I got a call from Ricky Ruiz, owner of the Double R Ranch. You mentioned talking to him about landing the account, but you didn't tell me just how big it was. He's excited to work with you, and he'd like you to bring the contracts to him to get them signed as soon as possible."

Rachel blinked. What on earth was he talking about? She hadn't even had the chance to speak with Ricky about the ad campaign, let alone pitch her ideas to him. Janie had said that both Ricky and Ty were excited about it, but instead of showing them her presentation, they'd sat through one about kidney donation instead.

"He called you?"

Dan nodded. "This morning. On my cell."

How could he sign contracts on something she hadn't even discussed with him? Rachel took a deep breath and opened her bag to pull them out. It was the company's standard representation contract, with some adjustments appropriate to Ricky's business. She'd put them in as a starting place for the discussions, along with a few mockups of ads as well as some of her ideas for the campaign.

The folder was gone.

She briefly closed her eyes, trying to think about what could've happened to it. She remembered leaving it on the coffee table in her suite so it would be handy to go over with Ricky when he found the time. But they hadn't found time. So what was Ricky doing with it?

"We hadn't discussed any specifics yet. I'm surprised he wants to sign the contract."

Dan shrugged. "He seemed very enthusiastic. He asked for a few changes, which is what I wanted to talk to you about. He'd like you to spend the rest of spring and summer at the ranch, to get a feel for it, which would make the ad campaign more unique to what he's trying to accomplish. I told him that he's not our only client and that you have other things to do, but he said if you were willing to come, he'd make sure you had a space to work at from there. I wasn't sure what to think, so I told him I'd discuss it with you and get back to him."

Ricky seemed to be doing a lot of arranging without having spoken to Rachel. Was this what having a family was like? People jumping in and getting involved with your business without even asking you? Technically, he had asked, but he hadn't asked her; he'd asked her boss.

But this didn't seem like Ricky's handiwork. "Did he happen to mention his lawyer, Ty Warner?"

Dan shrugged. "He was on the call."

Of course he was. The whole thing had probably been Ty's idea.

"I'm flattered, but like you said, I do have other clients. And I should probably disclose that there might be a potential conflict of interest. I recently found out that Ricky is my long-lost grandfather. His motivation is likcly more about getting to know me as opposed to wanting our business."

It was the ethical thing to do. Certainly more ethical than Ty and Ricky calling up her boss and asking if she could spend the summer at the ranch without asking her first.

Dan nodded. "Ricky said that, as well. I think he was

hoping to play on my sympathies for an old man wanting to get to know his granddaughter. I respect that. The question is: Do you want to go? You already work from home on the days when you have your medical appointments, and you've kept up on your work. That's not my concern. I don't want you to feel pressured into going out there if you don't want to."

That was what she liked about Dan. He'd always been good about letting things be her decision. When she'd gone back to work after leaving Chris, he'd stood by her and refused to let Chris's bullying tactics work. Chris had even threatened to ruin Dan's business if he kept Rachel employed. Dan had told him to get lost.

For the first time she realized that as much as she had always told herself she'd been completely alone during the situation with Chris, she had had someone looking out for her. Dan had given her a job and let her keep it when everyone else had turned their backs on her because of him.

Janie had told her that maybe instead of looking for everyone to let her down, she should look around and see how people had actually been there for her. Like God. That maybe some of the ways in which she felt she'd been let down by God were actually places where God had been taking care of her in ways she hadn't recognized.

Like with her job.

"I appreciate that," she said. "To be honest, I'm a little baffled that they're so eager to work with me when they were so busy with other things that we never had much of a chance to talk about it."

Dan nodded. "The kidney donation project."

They'd told him that, too? Dan knew she had medical issues, but she hadn't told him about needing a transplant. One more thing she knew she needed to do sometime soon, but hadn't gotten around to it. Legally, her job would be safe and she had plenty of short-term disability coverage. But for some reason she hadn't been able to tell him.

"Why didn't you tell me you needed a kidney?" Dan asked.

Because she didn't tell anyone much of anything, let alone her boss. Maybe, as much as she had been feeling alone in everything, some of this was her fault.

"I don't know," she said. "I'm starting to realize how much I shut people out. After everything with Chris, I was afraid to trust people."

At least that much she knew he'd understand. She hadn't told him everything about the situation, but he had seen enough.

"I guess I would have thought that you would have known I'd have your back." Dan gestured around the empty office. "A lot of people here would have. I know you're focused on raising your daughter so you don't socialize with everyone outside of work, but you have to know that many of your coworkers see you as a friend. Someone they care about. Brenda and I care about you."

Dan's wife, Brenda, often invited them to spend the holidays at their house. Rachel had always refused, not wanting to intrude or be a bother. But the sincerity in Dan's eyes made her feel guilty for those refusals.

"I'm sorry. I didn't realize. I guess I thought—" She shook her head. "I don't know what I thought. Other than I didn't want to be a bother. I promise I'll do better in the future."

The warm smile Dan gave her brought tears to her eyes. "First of all, you can tell me how you really feel about taking on the ranch account and spending the summer out there. After that, I would like to know more about your kidney situation, and more specifically, how I can be tested to be a donor. I haven't asked about your medical issues because I know they're protected under privacy rules. You don't have to tell me anything if you don't want to."

He wanted to get tested? It hadn't even occurred to her that Dan, or anyone else currently in her life, would be willing to make such a sacrifice. But she had also been surprised by how many people at the barbecue had signed up for more information on becoming a kidney donor.

Had she been underestimating people?

Rachel took a deep breath and, as she had been starting to do regularly since talking to Janie, she said a prayer that God would show her the right thing to do, and give her the right things to say.

Yes, technically, she didn't have to tell Dan anything. She'd only given the bare minimum information about her medical situation to protect her privacy, but also because she didn't think anyone would care. And yet, as Dan stood there in her office, she could see that he did care. All these years, he'd been offering her friendship, as had his wife, and she hadn't been able to see it. She'd been too afraid after everything that had happened with Chris.

She explained more about her kidney problems, basic

information she'd lived with for months now, but was brand-new to him.

When she was finished, Dan said, "So that's why they were asking about what it would cost to put ads in major publications about kidney donation. Ricky said he would spare no expense, but I told him I didn't think this was the most effective method. We brainstormed some ideas, and I hope you don't mind, but he said he would rather me handle this one and keep you on the ranch account, because he says you're too modest to ask for help for yourself."

It wasn't so much modesty, but that she didn't think anyone would be interested.

Then Dan gave her a sad look. "I hate to say it, but I agree with him. I know you are a private person, and I've always respected your privacy. But we can't just let you die because you refuse to ask for help. My conversation with them made me realize that you're likely not the only person unwilling to make your condition known. So I hope it will make you feel better that we're not just doing a campaign to help you, but to raise awareness about kidney donation so that others may also receive the gift of life. Besides, Katie deserves to grow up with her mother."

Tears sprang to her eyes. She hadn't considered the impact of her illness on others, except for Katie. Dan, too, understood how important this was for Katie, and she wished she could go back in time to that first Thanksgiving she spent alone, when Dan and Brenda had done everything they could to try talking her into going to their house, but she'd adamantly refused.

She thought about the warm community in Columbine Springs, and how they'd all come around her, but the real relationship had developed because she'd chosen to open up to Janie. She'd found a friend because she'd taken a chance, and maybe, if she'd taken more chances, her life might not be so lonely.

Ty's image sprang to mind as she realized just how much she'd done to push everyone out of her life. She hadn't given him a real chance, even though he had been trying to make up for how badly he'd treated her when she'd first arrived. Every time she felt herself softening toward him, she'd found a reason to shove him away.

Even now, as part of her wanted to point out the fact that Ty's interference here with her job was one more reason she couldn't trust him because of how controlling he was, a tiny voice inside her suggested that perhaps it was because Ty cared. Even though she also didn't like Ricky's interference, she'd already accepted it with the realization that he was only trying to keep her, the granddaughter he'd just found, alive. But she wasn't attracted to Ricky.

And maybe that was the real problem.

It had been so long since she'd been attracted to anyone that the thought of potentially giving her heart away and getting hurt again was too much to bear. She'd spent the past few years doing everything she could to keep from getting hurt, and now, because of it, she'd almost missed out on the opportunity to potentially find someone who could donate a kidney to her.

"I'm sorry," she said, hoping Dan could hear the sincerity in her voice. "I didn't realize until now how much I've been shutting everyone out. And you're right—

highlighting my need for a kidney just might give someone else the chance at life. I was so busy worrying about myself that I didn't think about others. I'll do better in the future."

Dan nodded. "We're going to make sure that you have a future. So tell me more about the ranch, so I can call Ricky with an answer."

As Rachel told him about the ranch and her plans for it, she realized that in a very short time, she had fallen in love with it. She could understand Ricky's passion for preserving it for future generations. And, as she remembered Ty's interactions with Katie on their hike and how gentle he'd been with her at church, she could even understand why Ty would work so hard to protect it.

Ty wasn't like Chris, controlling things for the sake of control. Ty worked to control the ranch because of how deeply he loved it. It didn't mean that she had to jump in and give him full access to her heart, but it did mean that she could give him a break.

"If you don't mind," Rachel said, "I'd like to call Ricky myself. I know his heart was in the right place, getting you on his side, but I think it's important we set some boundaries. I'm glad things are out in the open, and it's good to know people are on my side. But both Ricky and Ty overstepped, and they need to know that it won't be tolerated in the future. I don't want anyone going behind my back."

Dan nodded thoughtfully. "I hope you know that no one had any malicious intent here."

"I do. And that's why I'm interested in Ricky's offer. I hated coming home, but it was necessary, both for work and my treatment. I'll need to speak with my doctors to see how going back and forth to Columbine Springs will affect my treatment, so I will need to come back to town occasionally. I can stop by the office on those days."

Already, she was thinking about how she could adapt her plans to make this work. Her doctor had told her that she'd be a good candidate for home dialysis, but she hadn't explored it beyond looking at the literature she'd been given. She didn't want to have a bunch of equipment at home that would scare Katie. But maybe, just like she should have opened up to others sooner, she needed to tell her daughter what was going on.

She'd avoided telling Katie about her illness, just like she'd avoided figuring out legal options to protect her daughter when she died, because of her fears. She'd once said that after Chris died, he would never control her again. But the truth was, the constant fear she carried was just his way of controlling her from the grave. She didn't have to be afraid anymore.

"I don't want you pushing yourself too hard," Dan said. "As I've told you before, your health is my number-one priority. Yes, I'm in business to make money, but what good is money if it's gained at the expense of those who have helped you along the way?"

In some ways, Dan sounded a lot like Ricky.

They discussed further plans about how to handle the transition of Rachel working from home or the ranch, and it was surprisingly simple. While Rachel did have a lot of meetings, they often did video chats with clients across the country. There was no reason why Rachel couldn't call in to those chats, as well.

But that left just one more item on the list.

Rachel picked up the phone and dialed Ty's number.

"When can we expect you?" Ty asked without even greeting her.

Rachel laughed. "A little presumptive of you to assume I'm going to say yes."

"Ricky gets what he wants," Ty said, but there was laughter in his voice, and once again Rachel could tell the genuine affection that Ty had for the older man.

She also noticed that Ty's answer was about Ricky, not him. "And what do you want?" she asked.

There was silence on the other end for a moment, then Ty said, "I'd like you to come. We didn't get much of a chance to talk when you were here."

She wasn't sure she liked that answer or not. But she also didn't fully know what it meant.

"We do need to talk about a lot of things," she said. "But most important, before I agree to come, we need to set some boundaries. I know you have Ricky's best interest at heart, and you mean well, but you can't do things like contact my boss or arrange for a community meeting about kidney donation without discussing it with me first. I don't like that you went behind my back, and if my being part of Ricky's life is going to work, then you need to stop that right now. From here on out, if it's about me or Katie, or affects either one of us, you talk to me first. Got it?"

"We were just trying to help," Ty said. "You've got to understand—"

"You have to understand that you can't go behind my back. If Ricky wants me to stay in his life, then there will be no more of this. If you can't agree to that, I'm sorry, but it's all over."

Ty sighed. "Why aren't you having this conversation with Ricky?"

She would, but she also knew who was likely the driving force behind it all. "You're the one doing his bidding. More important, he listens to you. I'm going to tell him exactly what I told you, but I want you both on the same page so that if you do it again you can't point fingers at each other. Am I clear?"

"Crystal," he said. "But surely you can understand someone wanting to help."

That seemed to be the message she'd been given all day. "I do understand, but in the future, if you're trying to help, clue me in first."

He didn't say anything for a moment, then he replied, "Okay. I see where you're coming from. This is new for all of us, and there's bound to be some bumps along the way. I'm sorry I overstepped. But don't be too hard on Ricky. He's spent the better part of thirty years feeling guilty for not being supportive of Cinco. He might be going about it the wrong way, but Ricky just wants to do better, and be supportive of you."

His words made her feel slightly bad for being so upset. It hadn't occurred to her that this was Ricky's way of making up for lost time. But Ricky also had to realize that overstepping in this way would only serve to drive people away, not bring them closer. Maybe they all had a lot to learn about what healthy relationships looked like.

"I get it," she said. "But now that we had this conversation, I hope you get it, too."

"I do."

She was surprised by the sincerity in his voice. Not

that she'd thought he was feeding her a line before, but it was almost like, as he spoke the words, he was making a solemn oath. Something about it was surprisingly comforting, and whatever misgivings she'd had about him earlier, she felt a deeper trust for him now.

But that still left one more important issue. The one she'd been thinking about on her way to work.

"I also wanted to talk to you about what you said to Katie," she said. "Yesterday, in church."

The silence on the other end made her think he probably didn't remember. Maybe it was insignificant to him, but it wasn't to her. "About not having a dad?" she prompted.

"What about it?" he asked. "I know it's natural for a child without a father to look to the men in their lives to be a father figure. But I think we'll both agree that it's a terrible idea for a couple to get together simply to give the child a father. I didn't want to encourage her with any matchmaking ideas."

That was what he thought she was upset about? Obviously, he hadn't learned a whole lot from his friendship with Janie.

"I agree with that part," she said. "But you had no right promising her to always be there for her. You don't know that's true. You can't make that kind of promise to a child. Especially my child."

"I stand by what I said," he responded. "No matter what happens, I will always be there for Katie. Twenty years from now, if she calls me out of the blue, I will drop everything to help her."

The passion in his voice surprised her. It was strange

to think that he would have this level of commitment to a child who wasn't even his.

"Why?"

Once again the air between them was filled with silence. She supposed it was a good sign that he thought through what he said, but it was also frustrating.

"I know how hard it is for Janie and Sam. Janie's biggest worry is what will happen to Sam if something happens to her. Yes, she has her family, but she doesn't want to be a burden on them. Katie doesn't have the same support as Sam, so it only seems right that if I can be there for her, I will. We have a summer camp for foster children at the ranch once a year, and I've always promised myself that if any of them ever came to us needing something, I'd do what I could to help."

The sincerity in his voice made her wonder if she'd underestimated him. "I didn't know about the camp for foster kids."

Growing up, she'd gone to several camps for foster children, and had enjoyed them. But she hadn't thought about what the experience had looked like for the people running the camps. She'd just figured they'd done it for a tax write-off or something. That was what she'd overheard one of the camp directors say.

"It's always been important for Ricky to give back to the community. When he heard there were foster kids in the city who never had the chance to spend time in nature, he made a point of reserving a week every year for them to come. I work closely with a lot of the charities in Denver to find kids who would benefit from the program."

He might be a lawyer, but it was clear he had a heart.

And suddenly, she felt guilty for making so many assumptions about him.

"That's a great thing to do. I'd like to learn more about it when I return to the ranch. And I…"

Would it seem weird to go back to the part about him wanting her to come to the ranch because they hadn't had much of a chance to talk the last time? She'd been so hostile, wanting to make her point, and now, seeing this side of him, she had to admit that maybe Ty was one more person she needed to give a chance to.

"I hope we can spend some time together," she said.

"I'd like that."

The promise in his voice gave her hope. One more source of support to accept. One more way to open her heart.

And suddenly, that didn't seem so terrifying anymore.

Chapter Eight

Having Rachel and Katie on the ranch the past few weeks had been a refreshing change for Ty. Yes, there was still the work, but having Rachel and Katie around brought a lightness to things he hadn't expected. He finished reading the contract for a new supplier and closed his computer. Ty smiled as he leaned back in his chair and looked at the pictures Katie had taped to his wall. Every day she came in with another drawing and a big hug for him.

As if on cue, the door to his office opened and Katie bounded in.

"Ty! Lookit what I made you!" She held up a necklace strung with macaroni painted in various colors.

Rachel followed, looking slightly frazzled. "Sorry. I keep telling her not to interrupt you when you're working, but you know how she gets. She's so excited when I pick her up from day camp that it's hard to keep her contained."

"It's no problem," Ty said, getting up from his desk. "I was just finishing up for the day anyway."

That was the other benefit of having Rachel and Katie here. In the past he'd find all sorts of excuses to keep working, anything to avoid having to go back to his empty cabin at night. It wasn't that he'd disliked his life, but until now, he hadn't realized just how lonely it was.

He accepted the necklace from Katie as he returned the big hug that had become part of his daily routine. "Thanks. I'll wear it to supper tonight. Are you guys eating with Ricky or did you make other plans?"

The tired expression on Rachel's face made him wish he hadn't asked. "I'm just going to have Wanda send up a tray. I didn't have time for my dialysis this afternoon, so I need to do that."

She'd made arrangements for a home dialysis machine, which meant she didn't have to go back to Denver so often, but the treatments often interfered with her ability to participate in activities. Still, having her here was better than her constantly making the drive back and forth.

Even with the treatment, Ty had noticed Rachel's energy levels waning a lot more lately. Though a number of people had been tested to be donors, so far they hadn't come up with a viable match.

He closed his eyes and said a brief prayer that God would find her an answer soon. Katie needed her mother. Ricky was becoming deeply attached to them, and Ty…as much as he was trying to keep it professional, he couldn't not care about her.

When he opened his eyes, they landed directly on one of the flyers from the kidney donation center. Which had been happening a lot lately. No matter where he put them, they always seemed to show up of their own free will in unexpected places.

But they were just papers. Nothing significant.

Still, the dark circles under Rachel's eyes told him that maybe he should stop waiting around for someone to do something and take action himself. Wasn't that what he was known for? So why was he so freaked out about this? Other than they would potentially be taking a vital organ out of his body.

But not so vital, since he'd still have a working kidney, and, if they were a match, so would Rachel.

He'd reread the material tonight. But for now there was a more pressing issue he could take care of.

Ty looked back at Rachel and tugged his ear. It was their agreed-upon signal that he was asking if he could take Katie without saying it in front of her and getting her hopes up.

He'd been spending more time with Katie lately, and while it felt good to know that Rachel was letting her guard down, it only made him more concerned for her health.

Rachel shook her head. "Katie is going over to Sam's in a little while."

He could tell by the fake excitement in her voice that she wasn't as excited as she was trying to let on for Katie's sake.

"Janie says we're going to make homemade pizza!" Katie's grin split her face.

"She makes good pizza," Ty said, smiling at her. "Can I help you guys get ready?"

Katie shook her head. "I've got all my stuff together."

A good thing, since Rachel looked like she was about to collapse on the spot.

"I can take her to Janie's if you like," Ty said, knowing she'd probably refuse, but he had to make the offer. Given the way she constantly refused help, not wanting to be a burden, he couldn't believe he'd once thought she was scheming to get Ricky's money.

Rachel shook her head. "It's okay. Janie is coming to pick her up."

The expression on her face made him think that she was feeling even worse than she'd let on. After all, she would have usually put up a fight at the idea of Janie coming all the way out to the ranch, not wanting to inconvenience her friend.

A commotion in the hallway made Katie turn and run out of the room. "Sam!"

Janie entered, shaking her head. "Those kids. I didn't think Sam could be any happier friendship-wise after Ryan moved here. But adding Katie has made them the Three Musketeers, and it's hard to imagine life without all of them together."

"She's never had friends like Sam or Ryan before. I see what everyone here means about lifelong friendships," Rachel said, a small twinkle in her eyes.

Even when she was this exhausted, she always seemed to find a small reserve of energy when it came to loving her daughter.

Janie laughed. "The boys were arguing the other day about which one of them was going to marry Katie, and they finally settled it by saying they'd take turns. I wasn't sure how to break it to them that marriage doesn't work that way."

Ty couldn't help smiling at the description. He didn't blame them. Katie was as adorable as a little girl could get, with the sweetest disposition. Like her friends, Ty looked forward to the time he spent with Katie. Rachel was doing well with her, and as he looked at the lines on her face again, he wished she'd let them all do something more for her.

Once again he thought about her need for a kidney. The doctors couldn't give them any information on potential donors until they were close to actually being able to do a transplant, but everyone they'd talked to who'd gone in for testing had said they weren't a match for one reason or another.

His conscience pricked him again as he thought about the card on his desk. Katie deserved a life with her mother. As it was, Rachel was already limiting her activities because she couldn't do as much as she got sicker.

Katie deserved better.

And as he watched Rachel and Janie laughing about their children's antics, Ty couldn't help thinking that Rachel deserved to have a life full of love and enjoyment. Her life had been so hard this far, and now that she was finally surrounded by family and friends who loved her, she didn't get to enjoy it the way they all would have liked.

Selfishly, as much as Ty tried not to think about it, he also couldn't imagine his life without Rachel in it.

Ty hoped that someday Rachel could accept the friendship of those around her without automatically being afraid that she was somehow intruding.

But that took time, something they may not have much of, if Rachel's current appearance was an indicator.

Rachel looked at the door. "I suppose we should go make sure the children aren't getting in Ricky's way."

Once again Rachel was worrying too much. Janie seemed to agree with him. She looked over at Ty, then shook her head as she turned her attention back to Rachel. "You let them be. I keep telling you I've never seen Ricky look happier. You have no idea the gift you've given him, so don't you dare take that away from him."

That same tired smile filled Rachel's eyes. "I'm glad. I just hate the thought of being a burden on anyone."

Janie put her arm around her. "Surely you've figured out by now that if you were a burden or bothering us, we'd tell you."

As they walked out of Ty's office and down the hall, the sound of laughter in the kitchen told them that the trip to the barn had not happened yet.

"There was an emergency at the bunkhouse Ricky had to deal with," Wanda said. "The kids were expecting something fun, so I couldn't disappoint them. I hope you don't mind waiting until the cookies are finished to leave."

Janie grinned. "As long as I get to bring some of those cookies home with us."

Running over to Ty, Katie said, "You should help us. We could make another giant cookie like we did the other day. Sam didn't get to try it."

Her enthusiasm brought a smile to Ty's face, but Wanda scowled.

"Not today, you're not," Wanda said. "You two make a

mess of my kitchen with all your crazy experiments. We're making normal cookies so Janie can take some home."

The worried look on Katie's face told Ty that she didn't realize Wanda was joking. He gave the little girl a small nudge and winked at her. "Next time," he said.

Katie's smile warmed Ty's heart, and once again, he couldn't help thinking of how the arrival of the tiny family had brought so much joy to his life.

Wanda looked over at Rachel. "You don't look like you're feeling very well," she said. "What are you thinking for dinner? We were doing the barbecue for the hands tonight, so I was hoping you would join us. But you don't look up for it. I've got some soup I can heat up. Leftovers from last night."

Rachel shook her head. "Actually, I'm not that hungry. I think I'll go upstairs, do my treatment and go to bed."

A concerned expression filled Wanda's face as she examined Rachel. "Are you sure you don't want anything to eat? You need to keep your strength up."

Rachel shook her head again. "I had a big lunch, and I ate late, so I'll be fine."

They chatted for a few minutes, and Ty found himself with the ever-present smile that invariably came with spending time with Rachel, Janie and the children. When the cookies were out of the oven and sufficiently cooled, Wanda put them in a container for Janie to take with her and the kids back to her house. Even though they'd told Rachel a couple of times that she could go on upstairs, she'd stubbornly insisted on remaining until Katie was gone.

As soon as Janie's car pulled out from the back of

the house, Ty turned to Rachel and said, "Let's get you upstairs and resting."

But Rachel surprised him as she walked over to the porch swing that sat nestled in the corner under the eaves by the private kitchen entrance. "It's such a nice evening, and I've been inside all day. I'd really like to sit out here for a while."

She collapsed into the chair looking weary, but the peace on her face made it impossible to argue.

"Mind if I join you?"

She'd already closed her eyes as she leaned back against the seat and was gently rocking. "Suit yourself. But if you're just here to babysit me, you go on and do whatever it was that you were planning on doing. I'll be fine."

She wasn't fine; any fool could see it.

But since she'd asked him to check his motivation, he did. And as he thought about all the possibilities of what he could do with his time, the idea of sitting quietly on the porch swing enjoying the calmness of the evening with Rachel was the most appealing.

He briefly stopped the swing long enough to settle in, and though Rachel didn't open her eyes, she let out a long, contented sigh.

As they sat there swinging on the porch, he looked out around him at the ranch. From this vantage point, tucked away from the main entrance and the back deck, this area was mostly used only by Ricky and Wanda and their closest friends as a private entrance to the house. He could see past the small kitchen garden Wanda liked to keep up with, to the fence that gave the family a small amount of privacy from the guests, and for a moment it felt like they were in their own insulated world. On the other side of the fence was the bustling parking lot, the lodge where the guests were mingling, and farther still, all the cabins and other buildings necessary for ranch operations. He could hear the activity on the other side of the fence but it was muted, and here, in this isolated spot, he felt a peace he wasn't often used to.

"I feel better already," Rachel said, opening her eyes and turning to him. "I know you keep telling me about all the wonderful places on the ranch you want me to experience because you love them so much, but I think this is my very favorite spot. Sometimes, after Katie goes to bed, I come out here and just sit, listening to the stillness of the night, praying and thinking about how grateful I am to see how everything has worked out."

Rachel had changed since coming here. Yes, she still worried too much about being a burden or imposing, and that she didn't belong, but she was family. Once again he realized he couldn't imagine the ranch without her.

It was as if his final excuses for keeping her at a distance melted away.

That Rachel was the old Rachel. She hadn't known God, and she hadn't known the welcome she would find here. Maybe she had been deceitful, but he was finding it harder and harder to muster the same resentment he'd initially held against her.

He reached over and took her hand. "I'm glad you found your peace here. You're part of this place now. I know I've already apologized for how I treated you in the past, but I just wanted to say once again how deeply I regret my previous actions toward you."

She squeezed his hand and smiled. "After seeing the operation, I can understand why you would be so protective. I was in the lodge the other day when a customer was trying to fake an injury. I think, if the man's little boy hadn't called him out on it right on the spot, you would have been hearing from them."

Ty groaned. He had heard from the man. But thankfully, all it took was for him to talk to a few witnesses and go back to the man to let him know that if he sued, they would file a countersuit. It was amazing how quickly the man's story changed.

There were dozens of men like him, all trying to get their piece of the Double R pie. But he could finally see that Rachel was not one of them.

"It's all part of my job," Ty said, looking over at Rachel.

The admission made him feel as weary as Rachel had looked earlier. Protecting Ricky and the Double R took a toll on him that he hadn't realized until Rachel had come into his life. In the interest of protecting others, he'd put such a barrier around his heart that he hadn't been willing to let anyone else in.

This time when Rachel smiled at him it was devoid of the fatigue it had previously had. Perhaps this place really was relaxing for her.

"I want you to know," she said, "I underestimated you. I've held a lot against you, because of the pain in my marriage. It made me doubt myself, made me doubt my friends, and with good reason. But not everyone is like Chris and the friends I used to have. Everything I see in you comes from a pure heart. You really care about Ricky and the land. You're not Chris, who only ever cared about himself."

It hadn't occurred to him that she would have made that comparison. Especially since he had so little in common with people like Chris.

"I'm nothing like him," he said.

"I know," she said. "But what I did know was that you were an attorney, and my experience with them hasn't been great. Some of the things you did that were controlling made it easy for me to think you were just like every other attorney I knew. In my experience, all lawyers have been self-serving and didn't care who they hurt in the process. I'm glad to be wrong, and I'm so grateful to have you in my life."

Her words humbled him. They were both guilty of misjudging one another due to past painful experiences. It was time for them to move forward.

Rachel didn't know why she was working so hard to spit it out. She'd been thinking about this for a while now, and given that she was feeling especially bad today, she needed to have this conversation sooner rather than later.

So far they hadn't found a donor. Not even a hope of one. Though Janie had been reminding her to keep the faith and trust in the Lord, Rachel knew that the Lord didn't always answer with a yes. Just look at Janie's mother, who was a good Christian woman, dying of cancer, and prayers hadn't saved her.

What if God said no to Rachel's healing?

All the more reason why she had to have this conversation with Ty.

Rachel had been praying about it, and every time she did so, Ty's name came to the front of her mind. As a lawyer, he was uniquely equipped to help her, to make sure Katie would be safe in the event of Rachel's death.

He might not have been willing to get tested to be a kidney donor, but he could still help Rachel. How could she hold his decision to not be tested against him, when the surgery would cost him so much? Her insurance would pay for of the transplant, but there were other costs to Ty, like taking time off from a job he loved so much. That, and she'd seen how he turned green at the mention of surgery.

Her doctor had told her that not everyone who loved her would be willing to be a donor, and that she needed to love them anyway. Not everyone was meant to be a donor. She'd learned in church that everyone had their own special gifts, and you needed to honor people for theirs.

Ty wouldn't give her a kidney. But maybe he could use one of his other gifts to help her.

"I need a favor," Rachel said.

The earnest look he gave her made her feel bad. "Anything," he said.

That was just it. This wasn't like borrowing a cup of sugar or watching Katie for an hour. But he'd been saying she needed to stop feeling guilty for relying on everyone.

"I need some legal advice."

He looked puzzled. "On what?"

Rachel took a deep breath. "I know everyone is praying for my recovery, but what if we don't get the answer we want? I want your help in making sure Katie is protected in the event of my passing."

She hated the way he flinched at her words. No one wanted to accept that Rachel might die, least of all Rachel. But it was a possibility they needed to face.

"You're not going to die," he said.

Tears filled her eyes. She thought she'd made peace with this idea, but hearing Ty's denial hurt in an unexpected way. She didn't *want* to die, especially now that she'd found so many reasons to live.

"None of us knows how long we have," she said. "Even if I didn't have the kidney problems, I could get hit by a bus tomorrow. I have nothing in place to protect Katie. Which is why I want your help."

That got his attention. "As much as I hate to admit it, you're right. So many people die without making their wishes known. We aren't promised tomorrow. I have a worksheet you can fill out regarding your assets and their distribution. I'm assuming you want them in a trust for Katie?"

Having him in professional mode made it easier. It didn't feel as personal, or as real, preparing for her death.

"I do," she said. "But there's one more important thing I need your help with. What happens to Katie when I'm gone."

The air between them stilled. It had become personal to him again. As much as she'd appreciated seeing professional Ty, knowing how he responded to Katie made her more comfortable with her request.

Since coming to the ranch, she'd appreciated Ty's

interactions with Katie. He genuinely cared about her, and it was clear Katie was crazy about him.

"Do you remember when Katie asked you to be her dad?"

Ty stared at her blankly.

Maybe it hadn't signified anything to him the way it had to her. But knowing that Katie would choose him made him a serious consideration in her mind. Especially since coming to the ranch, Rachel had observed Ty with Katie and other children, and he seemed to have a genuinely loving heart toward them. More than that, Katie was always seeking Ty out, and when Rachel wasn't feeling well, Ty would help with Katie.

"You told Katie that you couldn't be her dad because it required us to be in love and married. But what about if I was gone? Would you be willing to be her dad if I weren't around?"

She couldn't read the emotions crossing his face. But then he finally looked at her and said, "You want me to take care of Katie if you die?"

Rachel nodded, still not sure if he was pleased or upset by her words.

"Wow." He closed his eyes briefly, like he was trying to process her words, or maybe he was praying.

But then he looked at her and asked, "Are you sure?"

Was he giving her space to take back her request? Once again tears filled her eyes, making her wish she hadn't said anything. But then he squeezed her hands gently.

"I'm honored. I know what a difficult decision this must have been for you. You know I would do anything for Katie. I just remember how upset you were when I promised Katie I'd be there for her no matter what."

She'd almost forgotten about that. "I was too hasty," she said. "I'm so used to people not being there for us that I thought you were making a promise you couldn't keep. But I know now that you meant that promise, and you will be there for her. My biggest worry with my illness has been not knowing what will happen to Katie if I die."

The concerned look on his face made her wish she didn't have to have this conversation. But that was the trouble with needing a transplant. She'd had to have a lot of conversations she didn't want to have.

"I see her here, and the community that has gathered around both of us. Katie has found a home in Columbine Springs, and if I can't be here to raise her, I know she will be in good hands. Ricky would do anything for her, and were he a younger man, I might have asked him, since he's family. But you're young, and even though we don't have any promises in life, you stand a better chance of watching her grow up."

She was babbling now, trying to explain the thoughts she'd had over the past month. But Ty nodded patiently, like he was trying to understand, process her words.

"It's a lot to ask, I know, but—"

His warm hands had never left hers, and yet the squeeze he gave her as he interrupted made her feel like she was firmly on a foundation she'd never before stood on.

"My answer was yes the moment you asked. Don't start telling me how you don't want to be a burden. Katie means the world to me, and my only hesitation is how unfair it is that you even have to face the possibility of having to choose someone else to raise her."

Swallowing the lump that had been growing in her throat, Rachel felt some of the burden she'd been carrying fall off her.

"I don't know what I would've done if you'd said no."

He looked at her with such intensity that she wondered if he could read her innermost thoughts. Now there was something she wasn't ready to confess. How her personal feelings and regard for Ty were growing. But she didn't have the right to say so, not now. Maybe not ever.

Did he see her as a woman to love, or a woman who might be dying? And was it fair to even ask that question with so much hanging in the balance?

"You mentioned the conversation we'd had earlier about me being there for Katie no matter what. I meant it then, and I mean it now. I will still be praying for your recovery, and I will put whatever resources I can behind it. Because what's best for Katie is her mother. But I'm grateful that you'd trust me enough to step in if the unthinkable happens."

She reached out her arms and hugged him. When he responded by holding her tight, she wasn't prepared for the flood of emotions that hit. She hadn't been in a man's arms since Chris, and Chris had never made her feel this safe, this protected. Actually, she couldn't remember a time when she'd ever felt like this. Ty was a rock, a foundation of goodness and strength who was promising to be there for Katie.

And a tiny part of Rachel wished that he was doing the same for her. That he would say the same thing to support her. Not that she was the kind of woman who thought she needed a man in her life. On the contrary, she'd always been self-reliant.

But here in Ty's arms, for the first time, she could see herself being okay with admitting that maybe she did need someone in her life. Someone to hold her, just like this.

Ty pressed a kiss to the top her head as he pulled away. "You know I mean that for you, as well, right? Katie isn't the only person in this equation I care deeply about."

Maybe he really could read her thoughts. Her stomach felt queasy as he examined her face.

"I…"

He smiled at her gently and, if she were to be so bold, lovingly. "Don't turn this into an argument, okay? If you're getting your house in order, then you have to let me do the same for mine. I know you don't have the capacity to process some cowboy lawyer making calf eyes at you. But I don't want either of us leaving this earth without you knowing how much you mean to me."

Ty paused, then he closed his eyes and pressed his lips together.

He was just as fearful as she was. Clearly, she wasn't the only one who had feelings for the other. But he probably also realized that this wasn't the right time for her to get caught up in some crazy romantic fantasy.

Then he opened his eyes and looked at her. "Sorry. God was just dealing with me on some things. I know I haven't shown my affection for you in obvious ways, and I've tried to give you space. You're dealing with so much that I didn't want to burden you with my feelings. So you don't have to do anything with what I just said. Let's just let it be for now."

This was why the whole situation was so difficult. Because there were so many emotions to sort through, and having Ty facing his, confessing because he didn't want her dying without knowing, somehow obligated her to be honest about her feelings, as well.

"I care about you, too," she said. "But I don't have the luxury of time to figure out what that means."

This was worse than being a teenager. Worse than being the naive college student who'd thought she loved Chris. She was nervous, scared and sick to her stomach, all at the thought of turning on an emotion she'd long ago locked away.

Ty sat there holding a key, and she knew that if she only said the word, he would open that long-forgotten room and maybe it would be safe to let herself love again.

"I'm not asking you to figure anything out right now," he said. "God willing, when you get your kidney, we'll have all the time in the world. But for now I want you to rest in the promise that I'm not just here for your daughter. Though I'll admit, I'd really love to kiss you right about now."

He wanted to kiss her?

Why did that make her more nervous than the fact that he'd just said he'd be there for her no matter what?

"I…"

Ty turned away. "It's okay. It was a dumb thing to say. You're not at a place right now where that was remotely appropriate."

Maybe not, but did she want to die without having

experienced the joy of being kissed by Ty? Being in his arms had been so wonderful.

What would it be like to sit here, holding each other, kissing and planning their future together instead of talking about what would happen if she didn't get a kidney?

That a man could know she was so sick and still like her so much—maybe it meant she should take a chance. Maybe something worse than dying would be to never know what it meant to be loved by a man like Ty.

"I'd like you to kiss me," she said.

He searched her face, his eyes full of questions. "Are you sure?"

Rachel nodded, leaning in to him.

Ty placed his hand on her cheek, cupping it gently as he came closer. "You have no idea how long I've thought about this."

She'd never been the type to make the first move or to go around kissing random men. But Ty wasn't a random man, and she'd never been so sure of anything in a long time.

As she leaned in to close the gap between them, Ty met her halfway, tenderly brushing her lips with his, and as he wrapped his other arm around her, drawing her closer, she wished she'd been braver sooner.

When she pulled away, she knew it hadn't been just a simple kiss.

They'd exchanged something very deep, something very special, and for the first time in her life, Rachel could actually believe that someone meant it when they said they'd always be there for her.

Chapter Nine

Whoa. Not that Ty thought of himself as an expert kisser, but that had to have been somewhere in the top ten of the most powerful kisses of all time. Kissing Rachel had profoundly changed something in him. It was as though his heart doubled in size, and all he wanted to do was keep her close to him.

After their kiss they'd sat on the swing in silence, Rachel resting her head against his shoulder, and Ty didn't want the moment to end.

When he and Rachel were talking about her future, he'd prayed for answers, and, as had been happening so often lately, he thought once again about donating one of his own kidneys to Rachel.

He'd been thinking a lot about the Bible verse that said there was no greater love than laying your life down for your friends. So wouldn't he be willing to donate a kidney for her?

The answer, deep in his heart, was yes, even if it cost him his life. Rachel deserved that. Katie deserved that.

While it was touching that Rachel trusted him enough to raise Katie, he shouldn't have to. Rachel should get to.

He wanted more moments like this, and if God wasn't willing to answer their prayers, at the very least, Katie could have her mother around to watch her grow up.

Rachel sighed contentedly, and he kissed the top of her head.

Lord, please give me more of these moments.

Part of him wanted to tell Rachel about his decision, but he also didn't want to give her false hope. He might not be a match. Several potential donors had been turned down, because while they were technically a match, they'd had other health problems preventing them from being a candidate.

Besides, something in his heart told him that this newfound conviction about helping Rachel was between him and God. He wanted to glorify God, not himself.

Rachel shifted, turning to look at him. "As much as I don't want this to end, I need to get inside and do my treatment. It's past time."

Before he could respond, his phone rang. It was Ricky's ringtone, so he answered right away.

It didn't take long for Ty to realize this wasn't an issue he could solve over the phone. Ricky was dealing with a drunk ranch hand and couldn't manage it alone.

"I'll be right there," Ty said, hanging up, then turning to Rachel. "I hate to leave you, but—"

She smiled. "It's fine. I'm going to bed after my treatment."

"Okay." He gave her a quick kiss on the cheek. "I'll see you tomorrow."

He went to the barn, where Ricky was trying to reason with a drunk ranch hand who'd been seen leaving one of the guest's cabins. It was too bad, because the cowboy was a good worker when he was sober. But the Double R had a strict policy about not getting involved with the guests, as it caused too much trouble when the guest left with a broken heart.

As Ty handled the paperwork terminating the ranch hand, he wondered how Ricky would feel about Ty becoming involved with Rachel. He supposed he should talk to the older man about it, but right now it felt too new, too special.

And yet, it was the right thing to do.

Once they solved the problem with the ranch hand, Ty walked with Ricky back to the main house.

"I need to talk to you about something," Ty said.

"Did you find Cinco's child?" Ricky asked. "I know you've been spending all your energy fielding calls about Rachel, but I hope you've had time for that, as well."

He hadn't made any progress on that front, though he had gone ahead and reopened Ricky's account on the DNA site in case a relative was looking for him. Not only would it potentially give them access to Cinco's child, but it could also connect them with donors for Rachel.

"No," he said. "Actually, it's about Rachel."

Ricky stopped and looked at him. "Not more bad news?"

"I'm interested in her romantically," Ty said, knowing that Ricky didn't like beating around the bush.

"Well, don't that beat all," Ricky said. "She's a right

pretty woman, if a man can say that about his own granddaughter. Smart, too." Then he looked Ty up and down. "I know I'm supposed to ask a man about his intentions toward my granddaughter, but I reckon I've known you long enough to know you'd do right by her. So what are you telling me for?"

Something about Ricky's words made Ty feel foolish for even bringing it up. "I guess, after what just happened in the barn, it occurred to me that it might be considered a conflict of interest to be involved with the boss's granddaughter. I wouldn't want to cause any trouble for you."

Ricky snorted. "We both know that what happened in the barn wasn't about falling in love. It was about a young man sowing his wild oats in the wrong field. It would make me the happiest man on earth to see you settled down with a good woman. For Rachel to have a man like you, that just doubles my happiness. When's the wedding?"

Maybe Ty had been a little too hasty in saying anything to Ricky. He should have known that would have been the older man's first question.

"Rachel and I both agreed that her health must come first."

Ricky nodded. "Is there any progress on finding her a donor?"

Though Ty hadn't wanted to get Rachel's hopes up, he knew that Ricky expected him to tell him everything. It seemed weird, keeping the information from her, but Ricky expected him to do everything in his power to make sure Rachel got a kidney.

"I'm going to get tested," Ty said.

He wasn't sure what kind of reaction he would get from Ricky, but a cackle wasn't one of them.

"You do love her," Ricky said. "I know how scared of needles you are. You turn white every time I mention you donating. Don't think I haven't forgotten the time we had that blood drive in town, and you took one look at the needle and fainted."

Ricky *would* bring up that moment of humiliation. But at least now he knew the older man understood what a big deal this was. He'd thought Ricky had been disappointed in him for not wanting to donate, but maybe it was just Ty being disappointed in himself.

"Rachel has a doctor's appointment tomorrow," Ricky said. "Wanda said she was feeling poorly earlier, so you could offer to drive Rachel into Denver, and while she's at her appointment, you could talk to the donor people about being tested."

It seemed like a simple solution, especially because it would give him the perfect excuse for being at the hospital without arousing Rachel's suspicion.

"Good idea," Ty said. As they rounded the bend, he caught a glimpse of the ranch house, or more specifically, Rachel's window. The light was out, which meant she was probably asleep.

"Just don't say anything to her. I don't want to get her hopes up. We've had too many potential donors not work out."

At breakfast the next morning, Rachel was surprised to find Ty in the kitchen. He was usually off checking on ranch business by the time she got up.

But the smile he gave her when she walked in the

kitchen made her realize he'd stayed behind purposely to see her.

Was this giddy feeling in her stomach what it meant to be really, truly falling for somebody?

She'd thought that what she'd felt for Chris had been love, but she'd never felt so happy to see his face as she was to see Ty standing in the kitchen, a cup of coffee in his hand, a smile lighting his eyes.

Closing her eyes briefly, she sent a silent prayer heavenward that there would be many more mornings just like this.

"Good morning," Ty said, giving her a brief hug. "I was thinking I'd drive you to Denver for your appointment today."

That momentary touch reminded her that the previous evening on the swing hadn't been a dream.

It was real.

"I hate to take you from your work," Rachel said, wishing she didn't sound so needy. Truth be told, she would like him to take her to her appointment. If only to have more precious moments with him.

He pulled her in close and kissed the side of her head. "I have business in town. Besides, I'd like to have some time alone with you."

Wow.

For the first time she could sense deep within that she wasn't a burden. All her life she'd wanted someone who didn't see her as an obligation, someone who truly wanted her.

Surely, if God could answer such big prayers for things she'd desired her whole life but been afraid to express, He would find a way to let her live.

"I'd like that, too," Rachel said, snuggling into him and breathing in his warm scent.

They talked the entire drive, and while none of their conversation seemed significant, what was significant was how Rachel's feeling of being fully accepted by Ty had grown. When they arrived in town, they still had an hour and a half before her appointment.

"Since we have time, could we stop by my office?" Rachel asked. "I don't have any pressing business, but it would be nice to say hi to everyone."

"Sure," Ty said. "I was going to suggest having a late breakfast or early lunch, but I'm not that hungry."

She wasn't hungry, either. The joy that filled her heart was better than any meal.

He turned off the highway and onto the road leading to her office.

"How did you know where to turn?" she asked. "I don't remember you coming down here before."

He shrugged. "I know the address."

It felt like he was hiding something from her. But that was probably a remnant of her past speaking, and the old fear of not being loved.

When they entered the building, Ty gestured at the coffee shop on the main floor. "I'll just be in there while you get your business done. Don't rush on my account. As long as we get to your appointment in time, I don't mind waiting here."

As they started to separate, Allison, one of the admins in the office, approached them.

"Rachel. So nice to see you. I didn't know you were coming back today."

She smiled at the surprised but friendly greeting. "I

had a little extra time, so I thought I would come say hi. And if Dan has a few minutes to spare, I'll check in with him, as well."

Allison looked over at Ty. "And who is this cowboy?"

They didn't get many men in the office wearing a hat and cowboy boots. Most of the men they encountered were all in suits, so she could see where Allison might be a little curious.

Ty held out his hand. "Ty Warner, head counsel for the Double R Ranch. And you are?"

Giggling like a schoolgirl, Allison said, "Allison Sargent. I work with Rachel. I've heard a lot about the Double R, but I think you are the first real cowboy I've ever met. So many wannabes here in Denver, it's a pleasure to see the real deal."

Was Allison flirting? And was it wrong for Rachel to want to punch the girl in the face for doing so?

But Ty gave Rachel a look like he found Allison's commentary annoying. "You'd be surprised at what a real cowboy does or doesn't do. There are a lot of stereotypes, and not all of them are true. For example, not all cowboys wear a cowboy hat. A lot of the hands on our ranch simply wear ball caps."

He sounded like he was doing a commercial for the Double R, which he probably was. Rachel couldn't help smiling at how Ty was always so focused on promoting the place he loved so much.

Allison giggled again. "Maybe I should come out to that ranch of yours and find out. Are any of your hands single?"

"We have a strict policy against our hands fraternizing with guests," Ty said.

With a pout, Allison said, "Oh, well. I need to hurry and find out what happened to the refreshment order for a meeting in an hour. They were supposed to have delivered the pastries by now, and they aren't answering their phone."

With that, Allison rushed into the coffee shop.

Rachel said, "I'm sorry about that. Allison's a little boy crazy."

Ty shrugged. "You go say hi to your folks, and I'll relax for a bit."

As she walked to the elevator, she saw Ty get in line behind Allison, and Allison turned to talk to him again. But this time she wasn't jealous, not with Ty's reassurances.

In fact, she felt light enough that she could have floated right up to the office without any help from technology.

Even though they'd agreed to hold off on any romantic talk because Rachel's health was a priority, spending time with Ty on the way here was making her think that maybe they should make the most of what time they had together. Hopefully, God would answer her prayers and give them more time than what she feared they had. In the meantime, she'd do everything she could to enjoy whatever she had left.

Chapter Ten

❧

Though it had been a few weeks since Rachel had made her decision to make the most of her time with Ty, part of her was already regretting it.

Time was running out, and while Rachel had been moved up higher on the transplant list, she knew that statistically speaking, more people died while waiting for a transplant than received a kidney.

As she cleaned the equipment in preparation for her next treatment, she glanced out the window to see Ty swinging Katie in his arms. A lump clogged her throat. She'd done the right thing in asking him to be there for Katie if something happened to her, but she hated that she wouldn't be there with them to enjoy it.

Putting the remainder of her equipment away, Rachel took a deep breath, trying to calm the frustration boiling up inside. Janie had told her that she liked to pray during those moments, when you had to face someone or something you didn't want to. So Rachel closed her eyes and said a quick prayer.

Though she didn't feel like there was an immediate

answer, she did feel slightly better knowing that she didn't have to have any of the answers. It was enough to share her troubles with God.

When she came downstairs, Ty was sitting at the bar in the kitchen next to Katie, who was dunking chocolate chip cookies in milk like any other self-respecting four-year-old.

"Hi, Mom," Katie said, turning to smile at her quickly, but then going right back to her cookie. "We're only eating one cookie so we don't spoil our supper."

Wanda entered the kitchen from the side. "Would you like one? I made a bunch for tonight's barbecue, and there should be plenty."

She didn't wait for Rachel's answer and went over to the platter of cookies sitting on the counter. "I also made my famous coleslaw, which is in your kidney diet recipe book." Puffing up her chest, Wanda added, "Well, not my recipe. That's a secret that's been handed down in our family for generations. But it's similar enough to the one in the recipe book that it should be good for you."

The support she was receiving from people like Wanda made Rachel even more grateful she'd come to the Double R. She hadn't just found a grandfather, but a whole family of people supporting her. Ty had been right. Family wasn't just about blood, but about the loved ones surrounding you.

It seemed wrong, somehow, that she'd only just found them and was already facing the possible end of her life.

Ty laughed at something Katie was saying, reminding her why she couldn't give up.

Wanda handed her a cookie, which Rachel gratefully accepted. Maybe she didn't have all the answers, but Wanda's baked goods were about the closest to a cure for most things.

If only a chocolate chip cookie could get her a new kidney.

Still, as she bit into the deliciousness, feeling the chocolatey goodness melt in her mouth, her problems seemed a lot more manageable.

"Mom! Hurry and finish so we can go play with Ty's dog. Ty says Bella's a cattle dog and has to learn to herd cattle, but playing fetch is good exercise for her."

"You should come," Ty said, giving her a smile that melted her heart like the chips in the cookie. "Katie has been having fun teaching Bella some tricks."

"Yes!" Katie jumped off the bar stool. "I'll even let you give Bella a treat when she's good."

Having just had a treatment, Rachel was feeling pretty good. Ty had been using working with Bella as a way to keep Katie occupied while Rachel had her treatments. They'd all agreed it was important to keep things as normal as possible during Rachel's illness.

The bonus of a dog to play with that Rachel didn't have to take care of made it a lot easier. If Rachel got better—no, when she got better—she'd get Katie a dog of her own.

"That sounds like fun," Rachel said. "I'd love to watch you train Bella."

They walked the short distance to Ty's cabin, and Katie flung open the door and called, "Bella!"

Bella came bounding out, and Rachel wasn't sure who looked more joyful, Katie or Bella.

"Mom, watch!" Katie used some kind of contraption to toss the ball farther than her little arm could throw.

While the ball was still in the air, Bella jumped and caught it, then landed perfectly before trotting back over to Katie.

"That's amazing," Rachel said.

Katie grinned, then tossed the ball again.

Rachel looked back at Ty. "I hope this doesn't take away from too much of your work. You used to always be so busy, and you've been traveling to Denver a lot."

"I remember what you said to me the night on the swing about priorities. I'd always rather be with you guys than anywhere else." The look he gave her made her feel so loved, it hurt to think that she might be leaving them.

"I'm glad we're making the most of the short time we have together."

He glanced over at her, then back at Katie. "There will be more time. There has to be. She needs her mother. I need you."

His words created an ache in her stomach. It was her daily prayer, but that didn't mean God would answer. And it didn't mean Ty got to choose how it all went down.

"But what if there isn't? Can't you see that I'm getting worse? Do you know how many people are on the waiting list for a kidney donor? How many people die while waiting?"

He glared at her. "You don't have to be one of those statistics."

She'd read about family members being in denial over the patient's illness. It had just never occurred to her that she would be facing this dilemma. So maybe, rather than seeing this as Ty's romantic rejection of her, it was more about his unwillingness to face her illness and the fact that they might not have any time.

"Someone has to be," she said. "Don't you think all those other families pray for miracles? Why am I so much more deserving of healing than any one of them? All I ever cared about was making sure Katie would be okay. Watching you with her and Bella, I know she will be. If I die, I have no regrets."

The look on his face told her that he wasn't going to accept her answer, but what other answer was there?

But before he could reply, a man stepped into the clearing. Rachel recognized him as Hunter Hawkins, foreman of the Double R.

"What's up?" Ty called out.

"Sorry to disturb you, but that call you were waiting on just came through to the main lodge. Sarah said you weren't answering your cell."

Ty reached into his pocket and pulled out his phone, then looked at it, a concerned expression on his face. "Thanks. I appreciate you coming out all this way."

Hunter gave a tug on the oversize backpack he was wearing, which was when Rachel noticed the little girl on his back. She hadn't socialized much with the single dad, who spent every free moment he had with his two-year-old daughter.

"Not a problem. We were just going on a hike to check the fencing on the north side anyway. You're on the way, and Sarah didn't have anyone free."

Ty walked over to Hunter and gave Hunter's little girl a tickle under the chin. Her belly laugh warmed

Rachel's heart, and once again she thought about what a great father Ty would be.

Katie also ran over to them. "Can Lynzee play with us?"

Ruffling Katie's hair, Ty said, "Not today. Her daddy needs to go check some fencing."

With a pang, Rachel realized just how much she'd already been missing out on in Katie's life because of not feeling well. Every once in a while, Katie chattered about a little girl named Lynzee, but Rachel assumed she was a friend from day camp.

"We could watch her," Katie offered.

Ty shook his head. "Sorry, but I need to return this call. It's urgent."

He waved Hunter off, then turned to Rachel. "I'm really sorry to cut this short, and I know you were saying something important. I wanted to at least acknowledge that, but it's all I can do for now."

As if this had happened before, Katie called out to Bella, who came bounding over. Katie gave Bella a pat, and the two of them walked to Ty's house, where Katie opened the door, let Bella back in, then firmly closed the door behind the dog.

"She's really good with her," Rachel said. "I somewhat regret not getting her a dog."

Ty shrugged. "She wasn't at first. Katie is good with Bella because she's learned how to be."

How could she be simultaneously angry with him for not addressing the issue at hand and yet have her heart melting at how much he'd invested in her daughter?

"I'm sorry I have to go, but as I said, it really is an urgent matter."

Katie came back up to them and took his hand. "Can I help?"

He smiled down at her, then shook his head. "It's grown-up stuff and I'm going to be holed up in my office for a while. But since your mom seems to be feeling good right now, why don't you take her to meet our new foal?"

He definitely had the magic touch with Katie, because her face lit up like Christmas.

Katie turned to her. "One of the horses just had a baby, and Ryan's uncle Nando showed us a special spot where we can sit and watch it so we don't spook its mother."

One more thing Rachel had been missing out on. Fernando Montoya was the ranch's horse trainer, and he was married to Nicole, one of Janie's good friends. Rachel had heard a lot about the Montoyas and had chatted with them briefly at church, but she hadn't had much of a chance to get to know them.

But as she watched Ty head toward the ranch house, the ache in her heart was more about the fear of not knowing how she was going to survive and Ty being completely in denial about it.

Ty couldn't believe he'd missed the call from the kidney center. It was killing him not to say anything to her, but he didn't want to get her hopes up. The doctors had warned him that because things could go wrong at any stage, it was best not to say anything to the recipient until go time.

But this—this could be it. Rachel's chance at a new kidney, and an improved life.

As he raced to the main ranch house, where he could take the call in the privacy of his office and had all the paperwork at his desk, he couldn't help thinking about Rachel's disappointment at him not talking about her fears.

But he couldn't. Not when he was working so hard to save her life. Not only did he not want to get her hopes up, but he also didn't want her to feel obligated to be in a relationship with him because of what he was doing. He still didn't know how he was going to maneuver that once the transplant was complete, or how he was going to explain everything that had gone into this process.

And then there was the call he'd been on last week. One more issue he was still trying to wrestle with. Putting Ricky's information back on the DNA website had yielded more results. Twins. Also the product of an extramarital affair. This news, however, was not met with joy from the other parties. Apparently, they'd given the test to their parents as a gift to track their family heritage, not realizing that it provided proof of an affair their mother had with a married man.

Ty had reached out to the twins to see if they would be willing to donate a kidney to Rachel, as well as have a relationship with Ricky, which had resulted in a number of angry conversations, threats of lawsuits from the other parties and Ty's throbbing head. He'd been choosing not to take any painkillers in case the need for his kidney became more dire and he had to be rushed to surgery, which meant he'd been spending more time away from everyone else dealing with his frustrations rather than taking it out on them.

While he knew he needed to tell Ricky and Rachel

about the twins, he was still working on gathering all the information so that he could present an accurate picture. They deserved to know that the twins existed, even if both men were insistent that they never hear from anyone associated with the Double R again.

But that was a mess for another day.

When he got into his office, he closed the door behind him and returned the call. His last tests had come back clear, which brought them one step closer to his being able to donate a kidney. Now they just needed to schedule him for his final psychological evaluation to give the whole transplant process the green light.

As he pulled up his calendar to check his schedule, Katie came running into his office.

"Mom's real sick," she said. "She fell down and hurt herself in the barn. She says she's going to be fine, but Mr. Nando wants her to go see a doctor to get checked out. You have to come and make sure she's going to be okay. Everyone listens to you."

Without looking at his calendar, Ty asked the woman on the phone, "When is your next available appointment?"

"Tomorrow afternoon," she said.

"I'll take it."

He quickly confirmed the details, then hung up the phone. Hopefully, he hadn't wasted too much time on the call. By the time he got out the front door, Rachel was already walking to the porch, escorted by half a dozen of the cowboys who'd been gathered in the barn.

"Not you, too," Rachel said. "I'm fine. I just got a little dizzy, that's all. I went to sit down, and I misjudged where the chair was."

Ricky must have heard the commotion, because he also stepped out of the ranch house.

"I'd feel a lot better if a doctor checked you out," Ricky said.

Katie tugged at Ty's hand. "Me, too. I came to get Ty to make Mom listen."

He hated the defeated look on Rachel's face. Her priority had always been about protecting Katie, and he'd done his best to help her with it.

Ty gave Katie a reassuring squeeze. "Your mom's a big girl, and I trust her to make the right decision. She'll see the doctor, if only to make the rest of us feel better."

He looked at Rachel, who mostly seemed embarrassed about the whole incident. He knew her I'm-not-feeling-well expression, and she wasn't wearing it. It seemed more that she disliked everyone making a big deal of the situation.

As Rachel approached, Katie let go of his hand and ran to her mom, wrapping her arms around her. "Please say you're going to see the doctor. Ty said it's the right thing to do."

Rachel hugged Katie close to her, but looked directly at Ty. "I see how you played that," she said. "And you're right. I will see a doctor, because it's the only way to get you people to leave me alone."

Busted. But it would give them all peace of mind, especially since he would have to drive down to Denver tomorrow for his appointment. If there was anything precarious about Rachel's health, he wouldn't feel right leaving.

Rachel's agreement was enough to get the crowd to disperse, and Ty escorted her into the family room, where she immediately sat in what seemed to be her favorite chair. Anytime they were in that room, Rachel gravitated to that chair.

Even though she'd said she was feeling fine, Ty couldn't help noticing that as soon as she sank back into the chair, she closed her eyes. Annoyance? Or fatigue?

Maybe a bit of both.

Ricky came up alongside him. "She looks just like my Rosie. I can't believe it took me so long to see the resemblance. I believe there has to be something of Rosie in her, since that was Rosie's chair."

Rachel opened her eyes and looked at them both. "Really? You've never said that before."

A tender expression filled Ricky's face. "Well, I'm saying it now. There are times when I look at you, and it's like staring right at your grandmother when she was younger. I wish she could have met you. You two would've gotten on real well."

"Tell me something about her," Rachel said. "A new story, one I haven't heard before."

As Ricky told Rachel the story of how he and Rosie had met, one Ty had heard dozens of times, he left the room to call the local doctor.

Once the doctor came on the line, he briefly explained the situation. Being in such a small town, they didn't have a lot of medical options, but this was always a good place to start.

"Let me talk to Rachel," the doctor said.

He figured that was where they'd end up anyway, given privacy laws, so he brought his phone into the family room and held it out to Rachel. "She wants to talk to you."

When Rachel took the phone, Ty motioned to Ricky that they should leave the room to give Rachel some privacy, but Rachel said, "No, it's okay. It's better that you're here to listen in so you know that everything's fine."

He was grateful, because even though he wasn't that worried, it was always reassuring to hear good news from a medical professional.

But as the doctor quizzed Rachel about what was going on, he could see the furrow in Rachel's brow deepen. It wasn't the reassurance he was looking for. In fact, it seemed like, based on the conversation, what Rachel said was nothing, might actually be quite serious.

Instead of giving the phone back to Ty when the conversation ended, Rachel dialed another number. "She wants me to see my doctor in Denver as soon as possible. I'll make an appointment for tomorrow."

Not the answer he wanted, but at least Rachel was taking it seriously and doing what had to be done for her health. As Rachel made arrangements with her kidney doctor to go in the next morning, Ty thought about how he could make getting her to that appointment work with his own. He'd asked for the first available so they could get moving on Rachel's kidney transplant. And now it seemed even more critical that he make it happen.

He just needed to find a way to get his appointment taken care of without telling Rachel what was going on and getting her hopes up. He'd heard stories about the operation getting canceled in the waiting room because of one failed test. How could he do that to her? At least they were both going to the same hospital, which made the logistics easier. Maybe he was making too much of it, but it seemed like Rachel had already had so many setbacks and near misses that it would be unfair for her to have to potentially face one more. Just because they were this close didn't mean they were already there.

Besides, it wasn't just Rachel's disappointment they'd have to manage, but Ricky's, as well. The older man had been following Rachel's case, and even though Ricky had been told multiple times that it was illegal to offer money in exchange for a kidney, Ty knew the old man would do just about anything for more time with his precious granddaughter.

He wasn't going to let anyone get excited until they were wheeling Rachel in for surgery.

So Ty prayed with all his heart that they'd get through this final hurdle, and that soon Rachel would have her new kidney.

Once the arrangements were made, Katie climbed up into her mother's lap. "You're going to be okay, aren't you?"

"Yes," Rachel said, looking at Ty.

He knew what she was reminding him of. If Rachel didn't survive, he would be the one to make things okay for Katie.

It hurt his heart that she had to go through this, but hopefully tomorrow's tests would be the green light they all needed to stop living in fear.

Wanda entered the room. "Ready for supper? I thought we'd eat with the hands tonight, so they could all see Rachel's doing better. Everyone has been asking about her."

Rachel hesitated, and Ty wondered if she really was

as okay as she'd been saying. It bothered him that despite all the progress they'd made in being open with one another, she still downplayed the times when she wasn't feeling well.

"Yay!" Katie said. "Maybe Hunter will be there with Lynzee!"

The little girl's excitement only made the pained look on Rachel's face worse. No, she wasn't feeling well.

"Why don't we have a quiet evening here instead?" Ty suggested. "I'll grab some plates for us from the barbecue, Katie can pick out the movie and we'll all sit in here and have some family time."

Though disappointment flashed on Katie's face momentarily, she ran over to him and wrapped her arms around his legs. "Even that horse movie you never want to watch again?"

Ty tried not to groan. Some of the kids in the youth group had recommended an animated movie about a mustang, and since then Katie had played it over and over. The last time they'd watched it, he'd begged her to never make him see it again.

But to give Rachel a much-needed break?

He scooped Katie into his arms and swung her around. "Even the horse movie, you little monkey."

Katie giggled, and as he looked around, the smiles on everyone's faces brought a satisfaction to him that he'd never felt before. He'd always known the love of a family, but he hadn't ever experienced the joy of seeing it grow.

"I really just want to go to bed and rest," Rachel said. "Why don't you take Katie to the barbecue and let her play with Lynzee? Maybe tomorrow when we get back from the doctor's, we can do something as a family."

It was unlike Rachel to be so open about how bad she felt, which meant she was probably feeling worse than she let on. But Ty was glad she was finally starting to trust them enough to admit what she really wanted.

He went over to her and gave her a kiss on top of her head. "If that's what you want. Can I get you anything before we go?"

Rachel shook her head. "I'll be fine. I'm just going to crawl into bed."

"It's my job to get you some food," Wanda said in a mock-stern voice. "I can heat up some soup for you."

The tender expression on the older woman's face reminded Ty again of how blessed he was to be part of such a great community.

But Rachel shook her head. "I'm really not that hungry."

Once they got Rachel settled, Ty and Katie walked to the barbecue with Wanda and Ricky. It warmed his heart to see how Katie had taken Ricky's hand and was chattering with him. Katie would be fine no matter what. Once again he prayed that God would find a way to make it true for her mother also.

At the barbecue, Ty tried to focus on having a good time and making things fun for Katie, but all he could think about was Rachel.

Katie grabbed him by the hand. "They're going to play music. Let's dance."

Ricky nudged him. "When a lady asks you to dance, you dance."

The music started up, and Ty smiled down at Katie. "All right, little one, show me your moves."

Giggling, Katie spun around as he twirled her. But instead of lifting his spirits, it only made him feel worse. Rachel should be here, enjoying this. Ty swung Katie around a few more times, but he couldn't get into the spirit.

Someone tapped him on the shoulder, and Ty turned to see Janie.

"What are you doing here?" he asked.

"Wanda called to tell me about Rachel needing to see the doctor tomorrow and asked if I'd take Katie tonight so Rachel wouldn't have to worry about her in the morning."

One more thing to love about their community. Even though he knew this was more about helping Rachel, it also let Ty off the hook for the night. He could get Katie situated with Janie, and then he could check on Rachel.

"I get to go to your house tonight?" Katie asked.

Sam came running over. "Yes! Mom says we can watch our movie again!"

A quick glance at Janie told Ty it was the same horse movie he'd almost been forced to endure yet another time. He'd have to get her something nice to thank her for taking one for the team.

"Why don't you guys stay here and enjoy the rest of the barbecue, and I'll go back to the house to get Katie's things," Ty suggested.

Not only would it give him the chance to check on Rachel, it would also keep the kids from disturbing her rest.

"Great idea," Janie said. "I see a tray of brownies calling my name."

When he got to Rachel's room, he knocked on the door softly. He'd noticed the light on through the window as he walked to the house, so hopefully he wasn't disturbing her.

"Yes?" Rachel asked, sounding wide awake.

"Can I come in?" Ty asked.

"Of course," Rachel said. "I'm dressed."

That didn't sound like a woman who was exhausted and ready for bed. When he opened the door, she was sitting on her couch, a bowl of popcorn beside her, the television on.

"I thought you were headed for bed," he said.

Rachel shrugged. "My show is on tonight. I didn't want to miss it, especially because they're about to reveal Damon's killer."

"But you said you were going right to bed," Ty said.

This time Rachel gave an annoyed sigh. "I don't tell you everything. This show is one of my guilty pleasures, and after hearing some of the people at church making fun of it, I haven't wanted to tell anyone how much I love it. You should've heard Janie go on about what garbage it was."

She lied to him over a television show? Lied to all of them. Made them worry about her. And over a simple thing she should have told the truth about. She knew how much he hated people lying to him.

"But I thought, after everything, you were finally opening up to me and telling me things."

Ty felt sick to his stomach. He'd prided himself on his ability to spot a lie, but he'd been so blinded by his growing feelings for Rachel that he'd missed her using not feeling well as an excuse to watch some show.

"I don't understand why you couldn't have just been honest with me."

Instead of agreeing with him and saying she would work on it, Rachel stared at him like he was crazy.

"It's just a show. Are you going to give me the third degree when you find out that I really don't like Brussels sprouts?"

"A lie is a lie," he said. "I wouldn't have judged you if you said you wanted to spend the evening watching your favorite show instead of Katie's movie. But you said you were going straight to bed. A relationship is only as good as the foundation it's built upon, and for me, the truth is very important."

Rachel shook her head. "It wasn't even really a lie. I did feel too tired to go to the barbecue. Is it so wrong to want to watch my favorite show instead of a movie I've seen a million times? I'd planned on watching it in bed, but I was a little hungry, so I popped some popcorn. I'm allowed to change my mind."

"It still feels deceptive," Ty said. "You don't have to keep things from me out of fear of being judged. If you're afraid I'm going to judge you, then we don't have trust, which means we don't have a relationship."

Instead of answering him, Rachel turned to the TV. They were talking about Damon's murder, which meant it would have more of Rachel's attention than Ty. It shouldn't matter so much, because he knew the show was important to her. But it stung to know that she was more involved in a television show than in understanding how hurtful her actions had been.

Maybe they weren't ready for a relationship. Rachel still obviously had to work through whatever issues she had about trusting him, even with minor things like a silly television show that people made fun of, and he had to figure out how much of this he was willing to put up with. When Rachel had deceived them into coming to the ranch, he'd had a hard time trusting her because deception was usually a pattern for people. He'd hoped that with Rachel finding Christ and realizing the importance of the truth, she would be able to break this pattern in her life.

But as he thought about how her lie—and more important, her justification for her lie—so easily slipped off her tongue, he wondered if this didn't point to something deeper inside her that God needed to heal before Rachel would be able to handle a real relationship.

A commercial came on, so Ty decided to give it one last shot. "I know you think you were justified in not telling me about the television show, but you know how important the truth is to me. You used our concern for you to cover up your true intentions. That's not how a relationship works. I need to know you're willing to work on this."

Rachel stared up at him. "And I think you're making too big a deal out of nothing. I feel like you're trying to control me with these demands. It's ridiculous that you're so upset over a small omission."

"You lied," Ty said, trying not to raise his voice.

"Maybe I felt like I had no choice, with everyone hovering over me." She squared her shoulders, staring at him like she was ready to fight.

But he didn't want to fight with her, especially since

it was clear she didn't understand how important this was to him. He wasn't going to be manipulated into believing twisted versions of the truth because he was blinded by his feelings. If she saw honesty as control, then they couldn't see eye to eye on the most basic value he held dear.

"Fine," Ty said. "I was just coming to get some things for Katie to stay over at Janie's tonight so we can get an early start in the morning."

Initially, he'd told Katie that she couldn't come with him because he didn't want her waking up her mom. But now...

"Do you want me to bring her up to say goodnight?"

Rachel looked away from the television and gave him a small smile. "That would be great, thanks. I was thinking I'd get to see her in the morning, but if she's at Janie's, I won't be able to."

Ty gave a quick nod, then went to get Katie. While Katie said goodnight to her mom, he packed Katie's things. He'd helped with Katie enough that he knew where her clothes were kept.

Katie grabbed his hand just as he was zipping up her bag.

"Come on! Janie said we have to hurry!"

He smiled at the little girl tugging on his hand. "You go. I'll be right down."

As Katie raced out of the room, Ty glanced over at Rachel, whose attention was back on her show.

She'd taken her eyes off it long enough to be with Katie, and while he couldn't fault her for focusing on her daughter, it hurt that he didn't get the same level of interest.

His heart shattered at the thought that fixing whatever was broken between them was less important to her than some fictional guy's murder.

At least he hadn't bought the ring he'd been eyeing. One less piece of evidence to his heartbreak.

Chapter Eleven

Rachel felt fine. Completely fine. So maybe she was
a little more tired than usual, but who wouldn't be with
all the stress? Ricky's doctor had recommended that
Rachel see her kidney doctor in Denver as a precau-
tion, and Ty had insisted on driving her. She'd tried
to think positive, that their time in the car would give
them the chance to talk. But so far she hadn't man-
aged to find a way to broach the subject of the previous evening's fight.

Ty had said next to nothing, other than to commu-
nicate the plan.

Which meant he was probably still angry with her.
She hadn't liked arguing with him last night, and she
sure didn't want to start another fight now. Rachel hated
arguing, especially with people she cared about. Sometimes it was just easier to give people the answers they
wanted. When she'd called Janie this morning to talk
to Katie, she'd mentioned it to Janie. Janie told her that
she needed to find a way to learn to trust people even
if it meant not saying what she thought they wanted to

hear. She'd even confessed about the show, and Janie had laughed. Even though Janie thought it was a dumb show, she didn't think less of Rachel for watching it.

"I should've told you about the show," Rachel said to Ty. "I didn't want you to lose respect for me, but I should have trusted you anyway."

Ty's grip on the steering wheel tightened. She could see his knuckles get whiter with the effort.

"I guess we have a lot to learn about relationships," he said.

The words were seemingly positive, but she got the feeling that her attempt at clearing the air didn't make anything any better.

"You're really upset, aren't you?" Rachel tried again to get him to open up to her.

"So now you want to talk," Ty said, not looking at her. "Because you don't have a more important television show taking up your attention. I'm sorry, but that doesn't work for me. I think we rushed into a relationship. I want things from you, like honesty, that you don't seem ready to give. You think that's controlling. So maybe it's best we take a break."

The way he said *take a break* sounded like his intentions were a lot more permanent than a break. Her heart started to crack into tiny pieces, and she tried telling herself that he was making a big deal out of nothing.

But this didn't feel like nothing.

"I need to get gas," Ty said, pulling in to the gas station.

She shifted in her seat, reaching for the bag of refreshments Wanda had so thoughtfully packed for them. Ty had already eaten his breakfast burrito, but Rachel hadn't been hungry, and even though she really wasn't right now, either, at least it would give her something to do.

As she reached for the small bag, she accidentally knocked over Ty's leather bag. Some papers scattered around the floor of the truck, and even though she didn't know where they belonged, she ought to at least pick them up so Ty didn't step on them when he got back in. He could reorganize things later.

But as she grabbed the first set of papers, she couldn't help noticing the names Alexander and William Bennett, listed as Ricky's grandchildren.

Why hadn't he told her there were more grandchildren? He knew how important it was to her to find someone who might be able to donate a kidney. After all, that was exactly why they were on their way to Denver. Because she was sick and needed help.

How could Ty keep this from her?

He was mad at her because he perceived her making excuses to have a quiet evening watching her favorite show as being lies, but he was keeping secrets from her that could potentially affect her life. Unbelievable. And to think she'd actually thought that she and Ty could use this time to talk about their relationship. Oh, there'd be talking, but she wasn't sure he was going to like what she had to say.

Ty entered the truck, carrying two cups of coffee.

"Sorry about that," he said. "John was trying out a new brand of coffee and wanted to know what I thought of it. He sent me with some for you to try, as well. You can have it before your appointment, right?"

He held the coffee out to her, then noticed what she had in her hands.

"What were you doing, looking through my papers?"

She glared at him. "I wasn't snooping, if that's what you're implying. I accidentally knocked over your brief-case and was picking things up, and I found them. How could you keep a secret like this from me?"

The most unbelievable part was that he was mad at her for going through his things.

"It's complicated," he said, putting the coffee in the cup holders on the center console. "To be honest, I wasn't sure how to tell you or Ricky. I was trying to find the right time and place."

Rachel shook her head. "That doesn't make it right. I thought you understood how important it was to me to not feel like you're always trying to control things. And the hypocrisy of you being mad at me over a small lie when this is something really big!"

He started the truck. "I didn't lie to you about this. I haven't told you yet because I'm waiting to have all the facts before sharing. It's the responsible thing to do with news like this."

His face was hard as he focused his attention on the road. He viewed her as the guilty one, and he didn't seem to understand what a big deal this was.

"They could be donors," she said. She hated the way her voice cracked when she spoke. He was mad about a violation of his privacy, which was purely accidental, when her life was on the line.

"They refuse to be tested," he said, his voice tense. "As a matter of fact, they want nothing to do with Ricky or the family. They're a product of an extramarital affair their mother had, and it's completely shaken their world to find out about their parentage. If you dig a little deeper in those papers, you'll find a letter from their attorney, asking us not to have further contact with them."

It was a lot of information to process, especially because the hurt in Ty's voice made her feel even more guilty for opening this can of worms.

This had been the exact problem in her marriage. When Chris had done wrong, he had always found a way to turn it around and make it her fault. Why did she feel so bad when she hadn't done anything wrong?

Then his words hit her.

"You asked them to be tested?"

Ty made a frustrated noise. "Repeatedly. I did everything short of begging them to come out to the ranch, and I would have done that, had their lawyer not contacted me."

He'd done that for her? Or Ricky? That was the trouble. It was hard to tell with Ty, and as much as the questions burned in her heart, she also wasn't sure how badly she wanted the answers. Still, if he said he'd done everything short of begging, she had to believe he'd really tried. Ty wasn't the sort of person to beg.

"Thanks for trying," she said. "I'm sorry for going through your papers. I didn't mean to pry. It truly was an accident, and I was only trying to keep them from being ruined."

Once again she felt herself falling back on her old patterns of behavior, apologizing to keep the peace when she really didn't have anything to apologize for.

Frankly, she was tired of always having to apologize. This wasn't all on her, and even though she wasn't sure she still wanted a relationship with Ty, if theirs was going to work—if any relationship was going to work—communication had to go both ways.

"But it was still wrong of you to keep this from me. Maybe if I had reached out to them, they would have been more open to being tested. Or maybe, if we all discussed it as a family, we could have worked together to solve the problem. But you thought you knew it all, and you didn't include anyone else."

The words came out in a rush, and she barely recognized her own voice. But she was standing up for herself, and it felt good. It didn't even matter what Ty's response was. She was standing up for herself, and for what was important to her. And if Ty didn't like it, then he obviously wasn't the right man for her.

"I did what I thought was best," he said. "This isn't just about you. I have Ricky's feelings to consider, too."

He still didn't get it. He was stepping in and making decisions for others without even consulting them. Why did she find herself so attracted to controlling men? Maybe this really was the answer she'd needed all along. Just because she and Ty had chemistry didn't make them a good match for one another.

But she couldn't just let this go. "That's not always for you to decide. Maybe you should talk to Ricky about these things, see what he really wants."

"Who wants to know they have family members who want nothing to do with them? It isn't as if he knew they existed. The Bennett twins, while they are Cinco's sons, are not Luanne's. It's just further evidence of what a lying, cheating jerk Cinco was."

The tension in his jaw made her want to comfort

him. Which made her feel ridiculous. Hadn't she just told herself all the reasons why Ty was completely wrong for her? What right did she have, feeling so much compassion for him?

Ty sighed, like he was carrying the weight of the world on his shoulders. And he probably was, taking everything upon himself and not letting others help. Funny, since that was the crime he often accused her of.

"He was really upset when he realized that Cinco cheated on Luanne with your mom. How do I tell him there were others? The more I look into the past, trying to find information about Cinco and Luanne, the more I think Ricky would be ashamed of his son. How do I break an old man's heart?"

She honestly didn't know, but it didn't feel right for him to keep so much from everyone else. Especially when it impacted them so greatly.

"But if you're keeping the truth from him, isn't that like telling a lie? If you hate lies so much, why would you let Ricky keep believing them?"

Ty didn't answer. And in the silence that hung between them, she had to wonder if she'd pushed him too hard. But she'd told him the truth, which is what he said he valued. And you couldn't only have the truth when it was convenient.

Just when she started to think they'd end up spending the rest of the drive to Denver in silence, Ty said, "I'm sorry I didn't tell you about the Bennetts. I thought I was doing the right thing in waiting until the right time to tell you. I'll talk to Ricky."

Rachel supposed Ty's apology was progress. But he also didn't sound convinced.

"Thank you," she said. "I know this is a learning process for us all, but you've got to realize the double standard here. You can't expect everyone to adhere to some crazy version of the truth without being completely honest with them."

"Maybe so," Ty said. "But you're just as guilty. Like I said, I'm not sure this is the right time for us to have a relationship. I have more important things on my mind right now. I hope you don't mind, but I'm going to put some music on for the rest of the drive."

He didn't wait for her answer as he reached for the radio and turned the dial to the Christian music station they liked to listen to. She couldn't fault his choice in music, though it was frustrating he didn't want to talk further.

"Fine," she said. "But I do need to know—are you keeping any other secrets from me? From here on out, everything needs to be on the table."

If Ty wanted their relationship to be based on honesty, then she needed a foundation of no more secrets. Maybe then she'd feel safe in opening up to him more.

For a moment he looked thoughtful, then he said, "I've told you everything I can."

As far as answers went, it wasn't what she'd been hoping for. But she supposed it was too much to expect a straight answer from someone who seemed to keep everything close to his chest. Definitely the lawyer in him. Still, it was a good warning that she needed to continue guarding her heart.

As far as failures went, this hadn't been Ty's biggest. But he also couldn't consider their conversation a success. He'd thought he was sparing Rachel from having to hear the hateful words from her half brother. He was angry and confused, and Ty didn't blame him. He didn't know how he would react if, instead of his gift of a peek into your genetic heritage, you found out that everything you believed about your family was a lie. Which was why he'd been trying to give the Bennett brothers the benefit of the doubt.

There hadn't been much time for patience, however. As he looked over at Rachel, the lines on her face spoke of exhaustion, even though she'd closed her eyes and appeared to be resting.

On one hand, he felt guilty for his answer to her. He didn't know how people who lied on a regular basis could do it. He *was* hiding something from her, and while part of him didn't want to tell her that they were very close to finding a donor for her as long as he passed this last test because he didn't want to get her hopes up, he also didn't want to tell her while she was angry with him. The last thing he wanted was her to forgive him simply because she felt obligated to him for being willing to donate one of his kidneys.

Besides, he still wasn't sure if their relationship could be salvaged. Yes, she'd apologized, but she didn't understand why it had been so hurtful to him. Which meant it was just going to happen again.

As much as he hated to admit it, she did have a point about not telling Ricky about the Bennetts. Ricky was an adult, and Ty needed to let him decide for himself whether or not he wanted to know everything Ty had learned about Cinco.

By the time they arrived at Rachel's office, Ty felt

good about having a plan, both for telling Ricky about Cinco and for letting Rachel know the last thing he was keeping from her. When he pulled into the parking lot he gently shook her awake, and when she came to, she had much more energy than he'd seen from her in a while. Maybe they had overreacted in insisting that she go to the doctor.

"Let me walk you in," Ty said.

"I'm fine," Rachel said, an irritated tone to her voice. This wasn't how he was hoping things would go. He smiled at her. "I know you are. I just wanted to let you know that I did think about the things you said to me. I know it seems like I was shutting you down, but I honestly just needed some time to process. You made some good points, and I wanted to let you know that."

She gave a tiny nod. "Thanks. I appreciate that. But I'd still rather walk myself in. I shouldn't be too long."

He watched as she walked into the building, hoping that what he'd just said was enough. She got halfway across the parking lot when a woman he recognized from his previous office visit stopped to talk to her. They both looked in his direction and talked for a moment longer. Then Rachel turned around and walked back to him.

Maybe she'd reconsidered his offer. When they'd spoken previously, the lady had seemed friendly, chatting him up in the coffee shop. He'd originally been thinking he'd go in and get himself something, but after the taste test at the gas station, he'd had his fill.

"What were you thinking, going to my office and asking people questions about me?" Rachel said as soon as she got to him.

"I'm not sure what you're talking about," he said. The lady had been asking him questions, not the other way around.

Rachel glared at him. "Allison said that after the two of you talked in the coffee shop, one of our other coworkers asked her about you because you had been at the office previously asking questions about me."

He did remember. Before they'd even had the paternity test results back, he'd made a quick trip to Denver to meet with his investigator and had stopped in the office to ask some questions of his own.

"Our coworker saw your notes. One of them was a section about me being an unfit mother. How could you think that about me?"

Of all the crazy things. Now he was defending himself against random office gossip based on something that happened months ago.

"Yes. I did look into that, when you first came to the Double R, because it was a huge issue in your divorce case. While I had absolutely no doubts about your parenting in the first place, it should please you to know that all of Chris's accusations against you were completely unfounded. I saw the reports."

Even though he thought his words were reassuring, they only seemed to make Rachel angrier. Her face turned a deeper shade of red than he'd ever seen on her before, and her eyes flashed with so much rage that if they'd been lasers, they would have melted him on the spot.

"Who gave you the right to do all that? And why didn't you tell me? You said there was nothing else you were hiding from me."

He hadn't known it would be such a big deal. "Everything that both me and my investigator found exonerated you. There are no skeletons in your closet. No one had anything but positive things to say about you. The only reason Chris's case against you got so far was because he was a master manipulator."

The look she gave him burned straight to his heart. "The only master manipulator I know is you. I can't believe I honestly thought that you trusted me. Only it isn't so much that you trusted me, but that your investigator couldn't find any dirt on me. I told you I didn't want any secrets, which in my opinion are just as harmful as the lies you so despise."

They'd already had this discussion, and she couldn't have driven her point home any harder if she'd put a stake through his heart.

"I'm sorry," he said. "I truly never intended to hurt you. All of this happened before we knew the results of your paternity test. When we get back to the ranch, I'll show you everything in my file. You can go through all my files. I meant it when I said there would be no more secrets between us. You just have to trust me for a little while longer."

The braying laugh that came out of her was a horrific sound that he hoped never to hear again. "Trust you? Ha. Maybe once I get the report from an investigator."

He'd really messed up, and he had no idea how to fix it. "If that's what you want," he said, trying to keep his voice even.

"I'll tell you what I want," she said. "I want you out of my life."

She seemed like she was about to say more, but a

strange look crossed her face, and then she crumpled to the ground.

"Rachel!" He ran to her, hoping she was okay.

When he got to her, she was unconscious, and he couldn't wake her. At least she was breathing.

As Ty pulled out his phone to dial 911, he prayed with everything he had in him, and he hoped it would be enough.

Why had he waited so long to decide to get tested? All of this was his fault. As much as he hated to admit it, Rachel was right. All the things he'd been doing in the name of protecting her and Ricky were just as bad as the deception he'd accused her of. He should have included them in the discussion about the Bennetts. He should have told Rachel he was getting tested to be a donor, and he should have kept her informed about how they thought he was a match.

Maybe it would have gotten everyone's hopes up. But maybe they could have all hoped together, and yes, just as Rachel had said, maybe they could have figured out different solutions as a team.

Ultimately, as much as he had accused Rachel of not trusting them, his words were merely a reflection of the problem in his heart.

He just prayed he wasn't too late in making the realization—and in getting a new kidney for her.

Chapter Twelve

When Rachel woke, she was in a hospital bed surrounded by beeping machines, and as soon as she moved, Wanda's face was immediately in front of hers.

"Good. You're awake. Take it easy, but there are some people who'd like to say hi."

Katie immediately grabbed at her. "Mom. You're okay."

Tears filled Rachel's eyes. She'd always hoped that her daughter would never see her like this. And now, with as much equipment as she was hooked up to, it probably meant she was so sick that she'd stay this way until she got her new kidney. If she got a new kidney.

Where was Ty? She shifted in her bed to look around the room.

She'd said some awful things to him before collapsing, and even though she was still hurt over his actions, she couldn't die with so much anger between them. She briefly remembered hearing him praying as she faded in and out of consciousness. She didn't remember his words, but she did remember feeling deeply loved and wishing, even then, that she could take back what she'd said.

She couldn't see him from her vantage point, so she twisted in another direction and immediately felt a searing pain in her side. But she could see, in the corner, his laptop bag. Surely he was nearby.

"Now, don't do that," Ricky said. "You're supposed to take it easy, and you could hurt yourself."

If Wanda, Ricky and Katie were here, it had to be really bad. Rachel turned to look at her grandfather. "Where's Ty? I need to talk to him."

Wanda and Ricky looked at each other, then back at Rachel.

"He's not here," Ricky said. "He had some other things to take care of."

Other things? Had she just imagined him praying over her? What if she had driven him away for good when she told him she never wanted to see him again?

"Can you get me my phone?" she asked. "It's important that I talk to him right away."

Once again Wanda and Ricky exchanged a look, then Ricky said, "He's not at a place where he can be reached right now."

That didn't make any sense, unless he'd gone back to the ranch. But why would he stay at the ranch while everyone else was here? Before she could ask any more questions, Janie came into the room.

"I just wanted to let you all know that—" Janie stopped and looked at Rachel. "Rachel! You're awake. That's such great news."

Even Janie was here. Now she knew it was serious.

"Do you know where Ty is? Ricky and Wanda are

acting funny about it, and I need to talk to him. I said some terrible things to him before I collapsed, and I need to make things right with him. I know I'm probably going to die soon, and I've made peace with that. But I need to make peace with Ty. I need to know he forgives me."

Janie looked confused. "Why do you think you're going to die?"

Rachel raised her arms as best as she could. "Look at me. I collapsed. I haven't seen the doctor yet, at least as far as I remember, but I already know what he's going to say. They still don't have a donor."

Janie came and sat on the side of Rachel's bed. "You don't know?"

Taking Rachel's hand, Janie continued. "Your new kidney is inside you. They found a donor. They were in the final stages of approval when you collapsed. It couldn't have happened at a better time."

She had a kidney?

"Who was my donor?"

Janie looked around the room. Then she shook her head slowly. "We're not supposed to say. The person wished to remain anonymous, but it's going to be obvious to you pretty soon. The donor was working on a letter to you to explain. But if you could just trust for now, it will all make sense in the end."

It already did.

"Ty was my donor, wasn't he? That was one of the last things he said to me when we were fighting. That I needed to trust him for now, and he would explain it all later."

Janie nodded as Wanda and Ricky came around her, Katie clinging to Wanda's side.

"He didn't want you to not be mad at him anymore just because he gave you a kidney," Ricky said. "Ty needed you to know that this kidney was no strings attached, so he asked us all to keep it from you until he could explain himself."

Wanda nodded. "He told us that if you figured it out, to apologize on his behalf and that in the meantime, you can have access to all his files so you can find out anything you want to know for yourself. I have a sealed envelope in my purse with a paper inside it that has his passwords. He said you can use the information however you wish, and that he meant what he said when he wanted no secrets between the two of you."

Tears filled Rachel's eyes. She'd completely underestimated him. Yes, she was frustrated at how he'd kept so much from her. But he'd actually listened when she called him out on it. And here he was, giving her a demonstration of how willing he was to work to make things right between them.

And for him to give her a kidney…

Yes, she could understand his not wanting her to feel beholden to him. He'd done his homework. You couldn't just make it happen overnight, which meant that he had been willing to make this sacrifice through the good times and the bad times that they'd shared.

Even when she'd thought he was angry with her.

He could have made the decision to back out at any time.

But he'd chosen to stay.

Just as important, though insurance would cover

most of the expense of the surgeries, Ty would have to take time off work, probably having to dip into his savings to do so. A huge ask for anyone. And he'd willingly done it.

Even with his explanation, he was putting the ball in her court and giving her control over where she wanted the relationship to go.

Which meant, even after all the things she regretted saying to him, he'd still been willing to go through with the surgery.

Ricky cleared his throat. "He also wanted me to tell you that I know about the Bennett twins. We talked about his investigation, and what information was best for me to know or not know."

The old man's eyes filled with tears, and Rachel knew that Ty had told Ricky the truth.

"I'm not angry with him for keeping it from me. Deep down, I knew all along. It was one of the things Cinco and I used to fight about. Not just whether or not bull riding was safe, but the fact that I didn't like the way he was carrying on, with all the partying and women. I clung to the good memories of Cinco, because facing the kind of man he'd been made me question what kind of man I was, raising a son who did so much wrong."

Wanda put her arm around Ricky and gave him a squeeze. "You didn't do anything wrong. You forget that I was on the ranch when Cinco was in his late teens. You tried your best. I used to sit on the porch with Rosie, telling her my fears if I ever became a mother. That if the two of you could raise someone who turned out like Cinco, what chance did Steve and I have? She told me that we do the best we can with our children, but it's up to them to make decisions for themselves. And when we finally did have our Grace, I learned she was right."

A tear streaked down Ricky's face as he hugged Wanda back. "I didn't know that about you and Rosie. She and I fought a lot about Cinco in those days, and I guess I always thought she blamed me for how he turned out."

Watching the healing happening between Ricky and Wanda over the past, and hearing how Ricky's own involvement with Cinco, his beloved son, wasn't so cut and dried, it made her again realize just how little credit she'd given Ty. More important, it made her realize how complicated relationships were. She'd always assumed complications meant they were wrong. But maybe it was working through the complications that made a relationship right.

As Ricky and Wanda continued their conversation about the past, they moved over to the small sofa on the other side of the room, and Janie took their spot, lifting Katie on the edge of the bed so she could be closer to her mom.

"I'll bet this is all confusing for you, isn't it, Katie?" Rachel asked. Her stomach twisted at the thought of how close she'd been to dying and how she hadn't done a good job of preparing Katie for it. Thankfully, it hadn't come to that, but her poor daughter must have been worried sick.

She was grateful that despite her own mistakes, Katie seemed to be doing just fine emotionally.

Katie shook her head. "Not really. You were sick,

so Ty made sure there was a way for you to get better. That's what I love about Ty. He always finds a way to make things better."

Funny how the thing that often annoyed her about him was one of Ty's best qualities. And how Katie, lacking the baggage Rachel had, so readily trusted him. Looking back, though, Rachel had to admit that what she viewed as being controlling was just Ty's way of making things better.

In some ways, Rachel had been just as controlling. In her desire to not be hurt again, she'd kept too much to herself, rather than letting others share her pain.

As she looked around the room at the people who'd shown love to both her and Katie, she wished Ty could be here so she could tell him how much she appreciated all that he'd given them.

She'd been wrong to compare Ty to Chris. Yes, they both could be domineering, but Chris had done it to make himself feel better, more powerful. Ty's motivation was always about helping the people around him. Chris had never intentionally helped anyone besides himself.

"If you see Ty, would you please tell him that I look forward to reading his letter?" Rachel asked Janie. "He doesn't owe me anything, but I would like to hear him out. And I would like to make amends for the harsh things I said to him."

Janie nodded slowly. "I will. I was just with him. That's why I came in here, to tell them he's awake and doing well. Just focus on getting better, okay? I know it feels like you have to take care of everything now, but you have time to work things out."

Maybe, but having been so close to death, Rachel didn't want to waste any more of the time she'd been given. This transplant was her new chance at life, when everything had seemed hopeless.

Now she just had to make things right with Ty so they could give their relationship a chance.

Maybe it was selfish of Ty to wait to see Rachel, but he'd been home from the hospital contemplating his next move for almost a week now. He'd given Rachel the letter, and he knew she'd read it, but they hadn't spoken.

He hadn't wanted to see her in the hospital, even though it nearly killed him not to. He didn't want either of them to see one another in a weakened state and have it affect the discussion they needed to have.

Which was why, as he relaxed in his dad's recliner, sipping a glass of iced tea, he was surprised when Rachel showed up in his parents' living room.

"What are you doing here? Shouldn't you be resting?" Ty asked. Rachel smiled, and even though he had no business admiring her, he couldn't help noticing how the color had returned to her cheeks. She seemed so much more peaceful and at ease than he'd ever seen her.

It was all he needed to see to know that giving her a kidney had been the right decision.

Not that he'd ever questioned it for a minute.

"That's what Wanda said when I made her drive me out here," Rachel said. "But I told her that if she didn't drive me, I'd do it myself."

Ty stared at her. "If I can't drive yet, then you can't drive yet. What were you thinking?"

He shouldn't have been surprised, since Rachel was

as tough-minded as a person could be. But his recovery was easy compared to hers, and her need to rest was even greater than his.

Rachel gestured at the couch. "Mind if I sit?"

He wasn't sure he had a choice, but either way, he didn't want her tiring herself out. He'd had the easy part of the surgery, and he wouldn't be running any marathons anytime soon.

"Sure. You probably already saw my mom on the way in, but if you want something, she'll get it for you. I'd do it, but every time I get out of this chair, she yells at me."

"And don't you forget it," his mom said, entering the room with a glass of iced tea for Rachel. "No matter how old they are, they're still your baby. Mine just had major surgery, so I am taking full advantage of the opportunity to coddle him as much as I want."

It was something that would have annoyed him in the past, but now he was starting to realize that everyone had their own way of showing love and needing to be shown love in return. If this was what his mom needed, then he'd give it to her. Now, if he could only find a way to give Rachel the love she needed.

His mom handed the tea to Rachel. "You just sit back and relax, and if you need anything, I'll be right in the other room. And if either of you overextend yourselves while you're supposed to be resting, don't think that I'm above giving either of you a good thump."

Ty grinned. "Thanks. I think we'll both behave."

He'd talked at length to his mom about how he'd messed everything up, and though she'd agreed with him that he'd been wrong, she'd also told him that it wasn't too late to fix things. He just didn't know how.

"You'd better," she said as she left the room.

When Ty looked over at Rachel, she looked a little scared.

"Your mom might be a small woman, but I'd be afraid of meeting up with her in a dark alley," she said.

Ty chuckled. "She taught preteens for a long time. My mom is tough as nails. But you're not here to talk about her. So tell me what's on your mind."

Rachel smiled at him, a warm, comforting look, one he would take with him for the rest of his life.

"I read your letter, and I decided that a response needed to come in person. I know you said that donating a kidney was something you thought was the right thing to do, and that you didn't want me influenced by that decision, but surely you can understand how it would influence me anyway. You don't just give your kidney to someone you hate, which means there has to be something there."

"I never hated you," he said. "Where would you get that idea?"

"I never thought that. I'm just saying things haven't always been clear between us," she said, looking nervous.

"It was all there, black-and-white."

Maybe it was dumb of him to say, but he also didn't want to put his heart on the line when he'd already done so and wasn't sure where Rachel was going with all this. Was she nervous because he hadn't made his feelings clear? Or had the space he'd given her made her realize that what she felt for him wasn't love after all?

"I know," she said. "And that's why I'm here. I have feelings for you, too. I just fought them for a long time because I didn't know what a healthy relationship looked like. I'd like to give it another try."

He thought about her words, and while they were what he'd been hoping to hear, he noticed how she'd opened with it all being about the kidney.

"I can't," he said. "Like I said, the kidney was no strings attached."

That was what he had to focus on. The discussion had to be about her heart, not her kidney.

"What if this isn't about strings?" Rachel asked. "When we left for Denver that morning, I had the intention of talking to you about making a relationship work. Only we fought before we could have that conversation, and I said some horrible things to you. I wish more than anything I could take them back."

The pain in her voice was worse than how he'd felt after his operation. Still, he had to understand the motivation behind her feelings.

"Why? Because I gave you a kidney?"

Rachel shook her head. "No. It was the first thought I had upon waking up, before I knew I had gotten the kidney, before I knew you made it possible. I didn't want to die with anger between us. The love I feel for you is stronger than any anger I had over you keeping things from me."

Ty took a deep breath. He'd had a lot of the same thoughts when Rachel collapsed. But mostly, he'd thought of all the mistakes he'd made, and how he'd do just about anything to make it right.

"I had some of those same heart-to-heart discussions

with God," he said. "Yes, you were wrong for how you treated me, but I also didn't do right by you in a lot of ways. I almost lost you. You were so close to dying, and I blame myself. It took me a long time to get on board with the kidney donation. Had I not been so selfish and afraid, you would've had a kidney weeks ago. But I'm just as stubborn and bullheaded as you are."

He'd said the words to God about a hundred times, and in his head a thousand more. But he'd never said them out loud. Saying them now, to Rachel, it felt like he'd lost a whole other part of him he'd been carrying around for a long time and didn't need.

Rachel leaned forward and took his hand. "Yes, but you always come around. You're willing to see other perspectives, and you're willing to learn from them. You're willing to meet me halfway, and you're willing to admit when you're wrong. But you also stand up for what's right, and I really love that about you."

She loved him. For reasons that had nothing to do with getting a new kidney, or a sense of gratitude. Still, she had to know his part in all this.

"You almost died," Ty said. "I know everyone is talking about how wonderful it is that you got your transplant and you're going to be okay, but I was there when you collapsed. I know the feeling of helplessness at almost losing you."

He hated the way his voice cracked. Maybe someday he could share this part of the story without almost crying. But he'd done it with Ricky, Janie and his parents, so he supposed it was only right that Rachel see his emotion, as well.

Rachel gave him an encouraging look. "But that's just it. I did get my kidney in time. I did survive."

"No thanks to me," Ty said. "I've wasted so much time dragging my heels on things related to you, and it almost cost you your life."

That was the part he was having a hard time getting over.

"So why are you dragging your heels now?" she asked. "You can keep fighting this, or you can acknowledge that there are real feelings between us, and stop looking at all the excuses we've both made and start asking how we can make this work."

Which was exactly the place he knew he needed to get to. Where he'd thought he'd gotten to. But now facing it in front of Rachel meant also facing where he'd gone wrong.

"I've spent my whole life telling myself that I don't need anyone, and then when Katie came along, I made my life all about her," Rachel continued. "But being at the Double R, being with you, has made me realize I was a fool for thinking that. I don't know how I did it on my own for so long, but now that I'm part of this wonderful community, I never want to be on my own again. I want to be part of the community. I want to work through things, because that's what happens in normal relationships."

He wanted all those things, too, and as he heard the earnestness in Rachel's voice, Ty realized just how much he had needed her to come into his life.

This was also about Ty being afraid of opening his heart and trusting. He put all the fear on Rachel, but the truth was, he was scared, too. And here was Rachel, offering him the chance to face his fears.

Not alone, but with an incredible woman by his side who would be willing to fight to make the relationship work.

"You're right," Ty said. "Doing everything on your own is a terrible way to live. I should know, because as you pointed out that day in the truck, I carry the weight of everything on my shoulders and I'm not good at sharing my burdens. But that's not how God designed us to live."

Another admission that made him realize just how desperately he needed Rachel in his life.

Rachel nodded. "Exactly how I feel. I once asked you to become Katie's dad in the event I couldn't be her mom. But now I'm asking you to join our family, not because I'm going to die, but because I'm going to live. And I can't imagine living without you."

Even though Ty knew he was probably going to hear some squawking from his mom at the sound of him lowering the recliner and getting out of his seat, he did so and walked over to Rachel, then sat beside her.

"Truth be told, I can't imagine living life without you, either. I told myself it would be enough to give you a kidney so that you could live and raise Katie, regardless of who it was with or where you were. But I was deceiving myself, pretending not to care because I didn't want to get hurt."

He took her hands in his. "I want to spend my life with you. Yes, I wanted you to live for all the reasons I've said, but I would really love for you to live so I can share your life with you."

The smile lighting up her eyes made all the pain, emotional and physical, worth it. No, he hadn't given up a kidney for her to have one so she'd want to be with him, but he had done it so she could live, and now she would—with him.

"Then I guess we're both on the same page," Rachel said.

The joy on her face was one of the most beautiful things he'd ever seen. None of the doctors' instructions on his post-op care said anything about kissing the woman he loved.

Ty put his hand on her cheek, feeling the silky softness of her skin and thanking God that despite all Ty's stubbornness, God had still seen fit to save Rachel's life.

"I love you," Ty said. "I know we just were talking about making a relationship work, but I would really like it if we were making it work in the direction of marriage."

Rachel giggled. "I kind of thought that's what we were talking about all along. But if we need to make it official, will you marry me?"

He grinned. "I thought I was supposed to say that. But since you asked, I sure will."

Rachel leaned forward. "I know what I want. And I'm not afraid to fight for it."

Just as he was leaning in to kiss her, she kissed him, and it was better than anything he could've initiated. Her touch spoke of absolute love for him, and as they kissed, he couldn't stop the overwhelming feeling of gratitude washing over him.

It hadn't been an easy road, and he'd almost lost her.

But he could either dwell on his mistakes or accept the gift she was offering him here and now.

He broke off the kiss and smiled at her. "Well, since you asked, I would love to marry you. I know we still have work to do, but I think we can both agree that we're willing to do whatever it takes to get through the good times and the bad. Together."

"I like the sound of that," Rachel said, bringing him in for another kiss.

Epilogue

The wedding was small, but it was everything Rachel could have hoped for. Just her, Ty, Ricky, Ty's parents and their close friends at the ranch.

They'd just finished with the pictures when she spied Katie and Sam arguing.

"How did you get Ty to be your dad?" Sam asked, looking angrier than Rachel had ever seen him with Katie. "I've known him since I got borned, and I've asked God lots of times to make Ty my dad. It's not fair."

The poor little boy looked like he was about to cry, but Katie put her arm around him. "I'm sorry. I didn't mean to steal him from you. But Ty loves my mom, so he gets to be my dad."

Janie must have overheard the kids, as well, because she stepped in. "I've told you lots of times that Ty and I don't love each other the way moms and dads do. We should be happy that he and Rachel found each other and that Katie finally has a daddy."

"But I want a dad, too." Sam's eyes filled with tears.

Katie gave her friend a hug. "Just like you were going to share your Poppa and Gramma with me, I'll share my dad with you. And, now that I have another grandma and grandpa, we can share them, too. They said they're excited to have someone to spoil, so they can have two someones to spoil." She looked over at Rachel. "Right, Mom?"

Rachel tried not to laugh, especially since Janie was doing her best to hold in her own laughter.

Before Rachel could answer, Ty joined them. "I have always promised that I'd be there for Sam. But I think it might be confusing to others if he called me Dad."

Katie ran over to him. "But I get to, right, Dad?"

The happiness on her daughter's face brought tears to Rachel's eyes. But they started to fall at the sheer joy in Ty's expression.

"You sure do." Then he looked over at Rachel, giving her the heart-melting smile she loved so much. "We're a family. Today just made official what we all felt for each other."

When they'd signed the marriage certificate, they had also signed adoption papers, making Katie officially Ty's daughter. And as Katie hugged her new dad, Ty held his arm out to Rachel.

"Come here. Let's make this a proper family hug."

Rachel did as she was asked, but after one tight squeeze, Ty opened his arm again. "Come here, Sam. You and your mom are part of our family, too."

Even though he hadn't needed to, Ty had made the effort to make Sam feel special on this big day. When they all finished hugging, Katie took Sam by the hand.

As the two children walked off, having seemingly

made up after their fight, Rachel heard Katie say, "And now we'll work on finding you a real dad, too."

It didn't seem like Janie overheard, which was probably a good thing since she'd sworn off men, but Rachel couldn't help adding a prayer of her own that Janie would find a love as deep as the one she'd found for herself.

* * * * *

Check out the series that first introduced the Double R Ranch and the town of Columbine Springs—Three Sisters Ranch!

Her Cowboy Inheritance
The Cowboy's Faith
His Christmas Redemption

Available now from Love Inspired!

Dear Reader,

A while back, a dear friend of ours became ill and needed a kidney. Ed did everything he could, including putting a decal on the back of his truck to see if people would be willing to donate a kidney to him. While that decal attracted national attention, the source of his new kidney ended up being another dear friend who felt that giving a friend a chance at life was the right thing to do. No, they didn't have a romance, as they are both happily married to other people, but Tara's gift has always sat with me as an incredibly loving act. Our daughters have all been part of the same youth equestrian organization for years, and while we aren't in a small town like Columbine Springs, our organization is like a family, and it's always been touching to me to see how we care for one another.

While I did take some artistic liberties with the timeline and romance, it was important for me to share, at least in a very general way, the inspiration I found from watching my friends navigate this incredibly difficult time. I hope you will also find this kind of loving sacrifice inspiring, because there really are heroes out there willing to give the gift of life to another.

Newsletter: http://eepurl.com/7HCXj

Website: http://www.danicafavorite.com/

Twitter: https://twitter.com/danicafavorite

Instagram: https://instagram.com/danicafavorite/

Facebook: https://www.facebook.com/DanicaFavorite Author

Amazon: https://www.amazon.com/Danica-Favorite/e/ B00KRP0IFU

BookBub: https://www.bookbub.com/authors/danica-favorite

May the blessings of the Lord be with you,
Danica Favorite

WE HOPE YOU ENJOYED
THIS BOOK FROM

LOVE INSPIRED
INSPIRATIONAL ROMANCE

Uplifting stories of faith, forgiveness and hope.

Fall in love with stories where faith helps
guide you through life's challenges, and discover
the promise of a new beginning.

6 NEW BOOKS AVAILABLE EVERY MONTH!

LIHALO2020

COMING NEXT MONTH FROM
Love Inspired

Available June 16, 2020

AN AMISH MOTHER'S SECRET PAST
Green Mountain Blessings • by Jo Ann Brown
Widow Rachel Yoder has a secret: she's a military veteran trying to give her children a new life among the Amish. Though she's drawn to bachelor Isaac Kauffman, she knows she can't tell him the truth—or give him her heart. Because Rachel can never be the perfect Plain wife he's looking for...

THE BLACK SHEEP'S SALVATION
by Deb Kastner
A fresh start for Logan Maddox and his son, who has autism, means returning home and getting Judah into the educational program that best serves his needs. The problem? Molly Winslow—the woman he left behind years ago—is the teacher. Might little Judah reunite Logan and Molly for good?

HOME TO HEAL
The Calhoun Cowboys • by Lois Richer
After doctor Zac Calhoun is blinded during an incident on his mission trip, he needs help recuperating...and hiring nurse Abby Armstrong is the best option. But as she falls for the widower and his little twin girls, can she find a way to heal their hearts, as well?

A FATHER'S PROMISE
Bliss, Texas • by Mindy Obenhaus
Stunned to discover he has a child, Wes Bishop isn't sure he's father material. But his adorable daughter needs him, and he can't help feeling drawn to her mother—a woman he's finally getting to know. Can this sudden dad make a promise of forever?

THE COWBOY'S MISSING MEMORY
Hill Country Cowboys • by Shannon Taylor Vannatter
After waking up with a brain injury caused by a bull-riding accident, Clint Rawlins can't remember the past two years. His occupational therapist, Lexie Parker, is determined to help him recover his short-term memory. But keeping their relationship strictly professional may be harder than expected.

HIS DAUGHTER'S PRAYER
by Danielle Thorne
Struggling to keep his antiques store open, single dad Mark Chatham can't turn down his high school sweetheart, Callie Hargrove, when she moves back to town and offers her assistance in the shop. But as she works to save his business, can Callie avoid losing her heart to his little girl...and to Mark?

LOOK FOR THESE AND OTHER LOVE INSPIRED BOOKS WHEREVER BOOKS ARE SOLD, INCLUDING MOST BOOKSTORES, SUPERMARKETS, DISCOUNT STORES AND DRUGSTORES.

LICNM0620

Get 4 FREE REWARDS!

We'll send you 2 FREE Books
<u>plus</u> 2 FREE Mystery Gifts.

Love Inspired books feature uplifting stories where faith helps guide you through life's challenges and discover the promise of a new beginning.

FREE
Value Over
$20

YES! Please send me 2 FREE Love Inspired Romance novels and my 2 FREE mystery gifts (gifts are worth about $10 retail). After receiving them, if I don't wish to receive any more books, I can return the shipping statement marked "cancel." If I don't cancel, I will receive 6 brand-new novels every month and be billed just $5.24 each for the regular-print edition or $5.99 each for the larger-print edition in the U.S., or $5.74 each for the regular-print edition or $6.24 each for the larger-print edition in Canada. That's a savings of at least 13% off the cover price. It's quite a bargain! Shipping and handling is just 50¢ per book in the U.S. and $1.25 per book in Canada.* I understand that accepting the 2 free books and gifts places me under no obligation to buy anything. I can always return a shipment and cancel at any time. The free books and gifts are mine to keep no matter what I decide.

Choose one: ☐ **Love Inspired Romance**
Regular-Print
(105/305 IDN GNWC)

☐ **Love Inspired Romance**
Larger-Print
(122/322 IDN GNWC)

Name (please print)

Address   Apt. #

City   State/Province   Zip/Postal Code

Mail to the **Reader Service:**
IN U.S.A.: P.O. Box 1341, Buffalo, NY 14240-8531
IN CANADA: P.O. Box 603, Fort Erie, Ontario L2A 5X3

Want to try 2 free books from another series! Call 1-800-873-8635 or visit www.ReaderService.com.

*Terms and prices subject to change without notice. Prices do not include sales taxes, which will be charged (if applicable) based on your state or country of residence. Canadian residents will be charged applicable taxes. Offer not valid in Quebec. This offer is limited to one order per household. Books received may not be as shown. Not valid for current subscribers to Love Inspired Romance books. All orders subject to approval. Credit or debit balances in a customer's account(s) may be offset by any other outstanding balance owed by or to the customer. Please allow 4 to 6 weeks for delivery. Offer available while quantities last.

Your Privacy—The Reader Service is committed to protecting your privacy. Our Privacy Policy is available online at www.ReaderService.com or upon request from the Reader Service. We make a portion of our mailing list available to reputable third parties that offer products we believe may interest you. If you prefer that we not exchange your name with third parties, or if you wish to clarify or modify your communication preferences, please visit us at www.ReaderService.com/consumerchoice or write to us at Reader Service Preference Service, P.O. Box 9062, Buffalo, NY 14240-9062. Include your complete name and address.

LI20R